One Hundred Days Hunting for Hugh

One mad Scottish woman

Locked in Australia

At home - alone

And a journey through a COVID lockdown with a very ~~un~~healthy obsession

Lee de Winton

Dedication

In writing my diaries initially, I pushed them onto social media and onto one Facebook page in particular; the Wrens page. I joined the Wrens many, many moons ago and even having left the Service in 1998, I still love the support the women of this organisation provide to each other. Each day there was unfailingly positive feedback, comments, and love. It really is these things that keep you sane during challenging times. This book is for them, Wrens, one and all, with my thanks.

And to my mother, Patsy. The amazing woman who always knows how I am, simply by what I write and never fails to appropriately intervene. She has provided me free good advice, nearly every day, almost every month, and certainly every year, persistently, since I was born.

Lee de Winton. Lt (Rtd), WRNS.

Foreword

During the dark days of Covid '21, working from home and living by myself, Lee's daily *dits* were the chance to laugh at the ridiculous. Some were so hysterical that I was brought to tears with laughter. It was a tonic that a doctor could not have prescribed. Thank goodness for the Military sense of humour.

Jacqui Lowman. Lt (Rtd), WRNS.

Preface

Since the commencement of COVID 19 much work has been undertaken into a better understanding of the impact on a variety of factors, but mental health was always my main concern. This affected individuals, their education, their work and society as a whole. There weren't many places in the world that didn't experience some disruption due to the pandemic. Figures subsequently released by the WHO quoted that the pandemic triggered a 25% increase in the prevalence of anxiety. I read those statistics and found myself nodding, the words silently passing through my head 'snort, like that wasn't expected' But some people; those who have spent time in various Defence Forces, serving world-wide, in isolated locations, limited social contact, limited time to speak to family, unable to get home easily, often confined to one location, sometimes to even a building...we knew. We knew how this was going to affect us. We knew how it would affect others. Did it then make us act differently? Did we go back into some survival mode? Maybe.... And I think this was mine.

In 2003, I served with the Royal Australian Air Force in Iraq. I was located in the Air Traffic Control Town at Baghdad International Airport. It was one building. One building in the middle of the airport. I stayed in one room. One room with thirteen others. We ate (and shared) Ration Packs. We called home when we could. We were isolated. My survival mode was to write a weekly email to a group of friends, and hope they took the time to write back, either by email or an actual physical letter. Mails days were so important. My mother looked at these e-mails as a way to monitor my mental health. When the humour was lacking in the emails, she knew the humour was lacking in her only daughter, her only child – and she would intervene. Twenty years later, I have decided to turn this story into a book. The aspirational release date is November 2024, and the title? **One Night in Baghdad.**

Details of this book, pictures and future books can be found on www.leedewinton.com

In early 2020, when Australia started to see the effects of COVID lockdown and all the associated restrictions, I was the CEO of Bankstown and Camden Airports. My Board at the time, correctly asserted their due diligence and asked me to look at deploying the staff to work from home. I pushed back and presented a plan that was well within the NSW Health guidelines that would allow the staff to continue as a group, supporting our aviation operational emergency services and airfield staff, whilst also supporting each other.

My main point to my Board was, I felt I knew the affect(s) of being locked down with greater or lesser levels of support; and trying to normalise what could be normalised in an abnormal situation, was paramount. They listened, asked many questions and ultimately agreed, as long as I was adhering to all the correct health advice and regulation. I have always appreciated that support.

In 2021, during the second large phase of COVID and its associated lock-down, I was undertaking an Interim role at a large Western Sydney Grammar School. Approximately 1000 students, over 150 staff back at school and a requirement for increased focus on the health and well-being of all concerned. The previous year seemed like a walk in the park with 20 people and 10 rooms. Then we hit the second mandatory lock down and for a variety of reasons, I was one of the first to go home – kicking and screaming admittedly.

Thinking back to those deployments and my weekly emails, knowing this time I was well and truly on my own, in my apartment, away from family, away from friends, I wrote a daily diary of my experiences and thoughts. This was undertaken with much sarcasm, a laser focus on the daily events, a lot of mirth and an unfailing desire to push the limits, safely, but at every opportunity.

This is my story of those few months.

If you are reading this and expecting over one hundred references to Hugh Jackman, and whatever saucy thoughts, I was having of him, you'll be a little disappointed. Whilst I started clinging to many delusions, and it helped me a lot, this isn't a filthy book about HJ. It's memories of COVID, just 'cos in twenty years, I won't remember any of it and probably neither will any of the readers. But you will eternally remember Hugh, because good grief, who could ever forget him?

Finally, I am Scottish. When I write it narrates in my head with a Scottish accent and I often feel like I am projecting that, sometimes forthright, blunt, risqué humour. When you read this, channel your favourite Scottish voice and overlay it. Enjoy.

Lock-Down-Under - Day 1 – A miss is as good as a mile

Photo courtesy of ABC news Australia

Oh, hello dear diary, my old friend,

To quote an old friend, you've got to be shittin' me! This whole series of unfortunate events was coming from one taxi driver not doing the right thing.

I looked back at the School Principal with what I thought was a steely eye glare and a resistant stance.

"Are you kidding?" I asked her. "I live alone. I am literally one meter inside the offending Local Government Area (LGA). One bloody metre, three feet. I could spit out of my window, if I were less lady-like, and it would be outside this zone. I don't take public transport and I am the only bloody one in the school affected! C'mon, let's take a risk-based approach to this! There is a school full of students and teachers here" Yep, I was on a roll. Indignant and ready to fight for my freedom; God, I am so so Scottish. Just missing half a face of blue paint!

She laughed at me and shook her head, "the Chair won't agree to breaking the rules, Lee."

It's not breaking them I argued, there are always exceptions for education, and this is an exception, surely we can rely on the exception, and as the Director of Operations for a facility this size, I think we easily fall into this. "I'm exceptional" I told her again – smugly grinning and what I thought was an exceptional play on words. See what I did there?

3

Again, she shook her head. Giggling like a schoolgirl instead of the impressive leader she is.

"I'll speak to the Chair" I said. But in my heart, I knew this was a forlorn hope. This made her laugher even harder. "It's your funeral" she shouted back, over her shoulder as she made her way to recount my tale of my woe to other members of staff that she knew would be equally as amused at my annoyance and imminent exile from the school.

Twenty minutes later, chastised and subdued, I was in my car, with whatever I would need, to run whatever version of school operations would occur, for however bloody long I would need. It was nearly my worst nightmare. I was about to be held in captivity, in The Playgirl Penthouse as I have named my somewhat beautiful, Sydney Inner South-West apartment albeit, for goodness knows how long. Alone.

Later that night, when I reflected on my old mantra; boasting that I would run out of toilet roll before I ever ran out of tonic water, I was beginning to wish I had packed some additional things from the school store cupboards. This was going to be a long few days.

A long few days. Indeed.

The principal called me later that night. She was still laughing with far too much mirth for my liking, sharing tales of glee at how everyone was highly amused at my disgruntled departure. She shared that the staff had said they were going to miss me, most especially the laughter that exited my office and found its way into every room in the Administration Building. Oh, and also that she'd been chastised by the Chair for not taking me in hand more firmly. The latter bit of information making me feel a whole lot better. But in her ever-cheerful style (something I adored about her) she intelligently rationalised that there weren't many up to that task, so she was in good company.

"Can I bring you anything?" she offered. Without missing a beat, my reply was "Hugh Jackman, have him stripped and scrubbed and sent to my apartment!"

She didn't hesitate either, now well used to my humour "... got enough wine?" I confirmed that I had, we said goodbye and I settled into my night, without logging back onto work. Bugger it, I thought reaching for a glass of wine. It was about then I realised there was some advantages to this working from home gig. No bra required, a short commute via the McKitchen and instantaneous access to wine at any time. It could be a lot worse.

Little did I know I was in for the long haul. Not a Melbourne long haul as that nearly lasted a century, but none less, it was the start of a long time alone. But with my sense of humour intact, I was ready to face it, one sarcastic comment at a time!

Lock-Down-Under - Day 2 – Ready for Launch

Dear diary,

Locked down and loaded! As the ominous shadow of lockdown loomed, I decided it was time to face the most pressing issue of our times – my car's unruly appearance (we all know how much I love that piece of metal!). While it might not be deemed a legal reason to leave home during the COVID era, I argued in my head that a bird had committed a crime of artistic expression on my vehicle that needed immediate attention.

With a level of determination only matched by my car's need for a makeover, I embarked on a rapid spray wish mission. Armed with a hose and bucket…nah, just kidding, I was armed with $5 in $1 coins and headed to the DIY car wash by the airport, where I attacked those avian masterpieces like a cape adorned superhero combatting graffiti. My wash bay neighbours watched in a mix of amusement as I engaged in a battle of soap suds and water, unsuccessfully dodging the puddles in my flip flops, swearing like the sailor I once was and the Scots woman I still proudly claim to be, all in the name of maintaining vehicular dignity during lockdown.

Also, the car wash wasn't in a lock down district, so that's legal, right? Yep, keep telling yourself this Blondie. Keep it up. What was it that we used to call it in Aviation Safety Forums? Oh yes, normalisation of deviation. Blast those compliance memories at a critical time like this. Blast them.

Having transformed my car from an avian faecal Jackson Pollock on four wheels, back to the black shiny chariot I love, I got into gear for battle, no time to waste, that toilet paper will be flying of the shelves. Again. Lockdown survival mode engaged and moving to hyper-drive, I was a blonde on a mission! Looking like a potential 100m sprint champion (a sight to behold, I can assure you), I made my way to the local shopping centre – battle ready was a phrase we used in Defence, well by heavens this was me today. I rode that cart like I'd stolen the bloody thing and some frantic shopping ensued as I loaded it with 'essentials.' For that you should read snacks and wine, cos they were going to be the essentials I needed to see me through this.

Being a long-time hater of grocery shopping and continually finishing it as quickly as humanly possible, I rushed through those aisles, with the finesse of a far more seasoned shopper, and one that was on a $1 million dollar timed-spend mission. I gathered canned food, tuna, noodles, comfort food as if preparing for the apocalypse. And of course, the all-important toilet paper, cos apparently, that's the gold standard of pandemic preparedness.

Ah, that old joke of mine, I would run out of toilet paper before I ran out of tonic water – well not in this century, baby! I was stocked up with both.

I left the shops, as triumphantly as a seven gold medal winner; with a cart full of provisions that I felt were, of course, truly essential; I couldn't help but feel a huge sense of accomplishment. 'I am done!" Lock down ready. Car washed. And armed with enough snacks for a Hugh movie marathon. Maybe X Men, the one where he has his shirt off, or are they all like that? Who remembers the story anyway in the face of that visual imagery anyway??

I was prepared. I was ready. I was stocked up. And I was smug. Whatever the stay-at-home Gods had in store for me, I was ready to face it head on. Little did I know in the weeks to come, my car's shine and cleanliness would be the envy of our apartment complex car park and my snack stash would become the stuff of legends.

Locked down, but certainly not out of style, humour, wine or imagination.

Bring it on my COVID nemesis – bring it on!

Lock-Down-Under - Day 3 – Just a bad tempered, lazy blonde

Dear diary,

Its only day three of lockdown but today is the death of good intentions; pave that road to Hell. I had been running the gauntlet early, I mean day one and two were filled with legitimate reasons to depart the Playgirl Penthouse and feel morally superior because I had a reason! Lots of reasons.

But maybe it was the imminent caging of the blonde heroine that prompted an absolute loss of one's shit at the opticians the day previously. Or maybe I'm just achieving a level of grumpiness due to my advancing age and lack of sex! Oops, did I really admit to that!?

However, the foolish, bald headed, skinny, mask wearing git that rudely pushed ahead of me in the queue, only to do a bit of tyre kicking (metaphor for wasting time, for those literal thinkers!) quite quickly felt the wrath of a woman on a mission with a timeline. Plus, I was carrying two heavy bags filled with red wine and tonic. So, I wasn't to be trifled with.

But today, the good intention to get out of the apartment for a walk this morning, went downhill when I heard the pitter patter of rain on the Playgirl Penthouse roof. Smugly I turned over in bed, buried myself under the 15tog quilt (smuggled from the UK on a previous visit) and figured another hour wouldn't hurt! But it did.

Trying to start work at 7.45am, having rolled out of bed ten minutes before, hair all over the place like a mad woman's custard, a computer that wouldn't turn on, people relentlessly trying to call; well, it was brutal.

It's nearly holiday for the end of term so the school is being sent home too. We always have a skeleton crew on site for deliveries and such like so time to address that and create a system for cover. It was 11am before I got off the phone, managed to make a coffee and changed out of my night, and into my day, working-from-home pyjamas! I was so worked up that I had to restrain myself from grabbing the red wine pre breakfast! But it wouldn't have been the first time I done that in life, I'll give you the tip!

Anyway, it was over 6.30 pm before I finished. Doesn't school finish at 4, I continually asked myself? But I was comforted in the fact one more day in captivity had passed quickly.

It's still raining intermittently so that's the walk buggered again. No restraint now. RED WINE. And where's Hugh? Let's have a look at that movie again. That'll fix it.

And soon I'll be heading to bed. I don't even care about changing into my night pyjamas!

Let's see what tomorrow brings.

Lock-Down-Under - Day 4 – When shit starts to get real

Grrrr, dear diary,

It's day four of lockdown and I'm thinking I have about four and a half months until I get to the stage of the same personality defects of having been held in captivity in that Baghdad Control Tower back in 2003.

After a FaceTube (yes, I know but I like to call it that) post on day three, I received some feedback from people who have done this for a year. Their thoughts are that day 1 and 2 are a write-off, it's all PJs, wine and Netflix; day 3 and 4 are the days where you should avoid sharp implements. Which is a shame as sliced carrot sticks and beetroot hummus are on today's list of snack foods. Then from day 5 you start normalising life in lockdown.

Anyway, after yesterday's disastrous attempt at morning exercise, I set the alarm for 6am. Yes, the road to Hell is once again paved with good intentions.

What's that I hear? Sounds like rain…. Yep, there it is. Low cloud, water falling from the sky, a grey colour is prominent – so what to do? Look, I could have dug out that calf length dri-as-a-bone waterproof jacket and a hat from some deep, dark cupboard and gone out but the call of the quilt and the pre warmed, flannelette sheets won out for a second day.

When I finally woke at 7, it was time to work.

Checking for any video teleconferences throughout the day, I smiled smugly and plastered my hair with a leave-in hair treatment. Time to get preddy. This working from home stuff may grow on me after all.

The morning calls started at 7.45 but by this time today, I'd had a cup of peppermint tea (a new addiction), my computer was warm and free of urgent emails as they were disposed of quickly, and I was ready to deal with the day. The morning calls went well and reverting to my Air Traffic multi-tasking training and experience, I also filed and shaped my nails. If this lockdown continues, I am going to have to revert to doing them myself so let get on with the preventative maintenance.

There are still some things that I am putting off. Switching on that hair removal Ooh, Ooh, Oww machine is one of them. I'm a single girl, so what's a couple of weeks of resembling a strategically shaved chimp – it is winter after all.

I haven't been tempted to reach for the red wine yet today, so clearly the day 3 and 4 danger zone may not apply to me.

The great news here in NSW is that 67,000 were tested yesterday and there were only 19 new cases of COVID and 17 had already been traced and were in isolation. There was also news of a party in the Eastern Suburbs where 30 people attended, 24 contracted COVID and the 6 that hadn't been vaccinated. So, whether you believe in vaccination or not, that's the today fact. I have previously used the medical treatment excuse to get out and did then follow it with a 5 km walk. Exercise, there's another reason you can leave your house. Bring on shopping Friday as I've already started my list!

Of note, Western Australia went into a 4-day lockdown last night and Queensland have just announced a 3-day lockdown from this afternoon. Interestingly the QLD Premier has just announced that she wants to stop International Arrivals coming into Queensland due to the risk. She is advocating for international arrivals to be held in Howard Springs, which is an immigration detention centre. I have no words. Oh, yes, I do. What on earth is the world coming to?

I really want our governments to look at how we do a COVID Passport. I want borders to open up again. I want to see my parents. I want the government to look at international travellers doing isolation/quarantine at home (if that's the case). And I want us not to be in this situation in another 12 months.

It's too long. Solo. It's going to be far too long.

Lock-Down-Under - Day 5 – Turning a deaf ear

Dear diary,

That's it, I am deaf. It must be an age thing; I am now deaf. I must be deaf. I'm sure I'm deaf. It absolutely has to be so.

As that's the only explanation for me to completely sleep through the 6am alarm this morning and not have to listen for rain as an excuse not to get out of bed.

To be fair, I did take the step towards the morning walk and placed the correct newly acquired clothing on the stool at the bottom of the bed. And when I get out of my PJs (estimated about 2pm), I'll seriously consider putting on the sports gear. It looks like the weather may clear and I may actually be able to get out of the apartment today, without getting wet. If not then, I'll consider the day PJs.... at this rate, noting washing day is Sat or Sun, I'll be at the bottom of the drawer and resorting to the little black number, normally saved for a special occasion! And there is no sign of the principal delivering Hugh to my door yet!

On a much better note, though. Yesterday's hair treatment came out well and so was followed by a toner and some time to get down and dirty with my new Dyson AirWrap. It was, admittedly, an extravagant purchase but since I have completely run out of space to put new shoes (and gin ironically) I looked for other avenues to treat myself.

Maybe I should just start clearing out some of the gin. One breakfast nip at a time!

Today continued well with IT and calls, there are always some pesky issues with work and the 1004 annual submissions that every school is liable for each year, but that's just time.

And today's COVID update for NSW – as I know that's what the thinking reader is after. Well, today was 22 cases and half are already in isolation.

Let's hope those figures decrease in the next few days. Otherwise, I'll be looking out for Christmas PJs!

Lock-Down-Under - Day 6 – Military Precision

Dear diary,

There is nothing like an old boyfriend contacting you on WhatsApp, from halfway around the world, to just check in on you and make you feel special during lockdown.

And what did I want or need? Well luv, you're in the UK with barely a passing resemblance to the one I want right now, so nothing you can provide! I mean it's pointless sending champagne or gin because, as we've established, I have nowhere to store it. However, the walk down memory lane of the good times we had was enough to brighten the day. And I remembered he did have a passing resemblance to George Clooney. Oh, for International Travel and a couple of hours with a good ex – sigh….

I knew I'd have to get out of bed at normal time this morning, and not repeat the rest of the week and avoid rising by listening for rain. I had an appointment for an ultrasound on my elbow and I was walking there. I had decided. No procrastination today. Nope, up and at em!

In complete transparency, I've visited that place before. It may not be on the busiest street in Sydney but it's pretty darn close and parking is always problematic or more aptly described as horrific. I really think that to get a parking space anywhere near there you have to promise your first born and since I am a childless, barren, spinster of this Parish (well divorced), I have no blooming chance. So, I was on a mission. No excuses and no thought to rain. I had even, once again, placed my walking gear (in the order you put it on) on the stool at the bottom of the bed.

I was ready.

Did I say, I was a woman on a mission? I am woman, hear me roar.

And so it began, I needed 30 minutes bed to door.
Five minutes coffee.
Five minutes shower.
Five minutes to get dressed.
Five minutes for make-up.
Five minutes with Dicky Dyson (so called for his four hot rods)
And five to faff around before I leave the house.
Rain or not – I was walking. I had my brightest shoes on!

It was raining…..

Nope. I am not being put off today. I grabbed the brolly, and I was out of the apartment. Despite some initial lift issues and so a mad dash down the seven flights of stairs,

I made the appointment (2.5kms away) with time to spare. I do however acknowledge that I need to work on my fast-walking skills, as at one stage I was overtaken by a grandad with a pushchair!

But I feel great. The damage to my elbow has now been assessed as minor and I did a round-robin of over five kms including the stairs to my apartment.

There is another aspect to all this though. I walked past shops today that I'd previously only driven past (and at speed; it is south Sydney after all!). One of which was a bathroom and tile shop. I have a bathroom; in fact I have two. And it would now appear one of which is about to get a makeover. Well, it was a nice-looking bath and there is that old boyfriend and of course Hugh. That bath would fit him perfectly....

And todays NSW COVID update? 24 new COVID cases with 12 already in isolation.

So, until tomorrow. When I have a day in the office. Insert excited scream here! Until tomorrow!

Lock-Down-Under - Day 7 – Day release

Dear diary,

Being the ever efficient, read compulsive obsessive, I laid out my clothes last night and set three alarms; such was the level of excitement I felt knowing that today I could actually **go** to work. I could wear clothes and shoes. I could do my make-up and hair for legitimate reasons. It was quite exhilarating. It was a breath of fresh air, literally and figuratively.

This massive seven days of lockdown has taken its toll and release has brought an overwhelming sense of joy. In fact, I haven't felt this level of pleasure since I divorced my first husband. And my second too, actually.

In NSW. COVID lockdown has four exemptions to leave the house:
Shopping.
Exercise.
Medical requirements.
Essential workers including education type shit you can't do at home.

On day seven, today Friday, I am due to be, at work alongside being actually, physically, at, at the school.

I should explain though that I am not a rule breaker by nature. In the spirit of the health guidelines, I created a roster for the team to come into work and catch up on any school admin unable to be undertaken at home, and I'd included myself on that roster. I took the input and feedback from the staff, who maintained that this admin-type of holiday tasks wasn't my job, and they were happy to come in and do it, but I mean, you can't let them have all the fun and freedom. No, no, what I mean is that as a leader and manager; you have to share the good with the bad and that now includes physically having to go into work. Yep, that's what I meant. I know its school holidays, but did I mention those 2000 plus submissions for attendance, financial and census type thingies that seem to be due NOW – well, this is where and when they get done.

Armed with a berry flavoured tea, I set off on the 23km drive to work and I was an excited woman.

I have to say, this is a big school and it's eerily spooky in a building with no other people. But that didn't last long as two ladies from my finance team came in about an hour later. They weren't due to be physically in school, and I was confused.

"What are you guys doing here?"
"It's bill processing day and more efficient from here with the amount of cross checking? You said we could"
"Was I drunk?"

"We asked early yesterday morning!"
"Okay, so it's a possibility!"

Anyway – there we were. Ploughing through work, with high levels of laughter and gossip in-between; whilst thinking and planning for an early, Friday combined with school holiday departure....

COVID NSW? A sad 31 cases today including a worker at an age care facility.

I'm not generally a pessimist but the numbers should have been improving by now due to the lockdown. I sincerely hope we don't go back to remote learning. However, it will solve one problem for me – I am short of a school bus driver for our fleet and recruitment is slow in this climate.

And me? Well today is shopping day, and my favourite Aldi is 500m from work, easier to park, is never crowded and very convenient. So, a good, no a great plan altogether for me to be at work today. Two birds, one stone. But I anticipate being back in those comfortable PJs by 5.30pm at the latest. The rest I will take from there.

Lock-Down-Under - Day 8 - Desire?

Dear diary,

You can't always get what you want. Or sometimes you just want what you can't have.

I have no idea why these two phrases have been swirling through my mind today. But if you know me and my already confused little mind, having more stuff in there, unanswered, impromptu thoughts, well, it isn't a good thing. My head is already full. In fact, it's in danger of leaking!

Well today is another day, and I was ready for it. Maybe my foray into work yesterday combined with the excitement of the weekly shopping trip into Aldi and dragging all my kill up to my apartment made me tired and ready for bed. I don't know. What I do know is, I was sitting watching World's Greatest Showman one minute and suddenly I blinked, and I was halfway through a Graham Norton Show. I am not sure how that even happened. But it was about 9.45 so I was ready for bed.

Now, having slept through nearly every alarm this week. I was looking forward to a great night's sleep. That 15-tog quilt combined with a grandma's feather bed mattress topper and soft fluffy flannie sheets.... it's like sleeping on air. And I was ready!

So, it was a little bit of a surprise that at 4am I was still awake. I tried; I really did. I tried the usual sacrifice to the sleep Gods, dark quietness, lavender oil, gentle music then I ended up watching the last few episodes of the Vicar of Dibley and a couple of really, really bad movies. In fact, one movie had Dougray Scott and Gordon Ramsay!! Yes, I'm not mistaken, and predictive text hasn't scrambled up the names, Gordon Ramsay, the chef, in a bloody film. And now in my bedroom; not a dream any girl wants. If at any time someone asks you if you want to see a movie with Gordon Ramsay - they are not your friend and you should run away, quickly! But I'm sure he's a great cook. He should stick to that and shouting at inept people killing their own respective restaurants.

Suffice to say, it was late (or early) when I finally went to sleep, not comforted by the fact I had a morning physio appointment! And I was darned sure I was walking to that.

As a result, today was beautiful here in Sydney. It was warm, sunny and it always feels like there is love floating around everywhere in the city on days like this. Look, being a single girl, looking for her next ex-husband, there isn't much of that love coming to me. I'm resorting to keeping myself metaphorically warm with thoughts of an unexpected visit by Hugh; that and more adorable messages from that charming ex in the UK! After all, a girl needs a hobby! Unfortunately, most of mine is in my imagination right now but a girl can have a dream.

Today's 45-minute walk to the physio was through Sydney Park, where there is no social distancing whatsoever! In fact, it's so bloody busy with people exercising that it may be necessary to walk on folks' heads to get through it. But it makes me smile to see so many people out in the fresh air. Out, out. Happy. Dogs aplenty. Sunshine. Smiles all around.

However, getting back to the fact that you can't always get what you want. I received a lovely email today from a stranger. And of course, I am relaying it for your amusement!

This opportunist is (or used to be) a connection on LinkedIn and managed to find my email there. Maybe he's a Nigerian Prince and I should send my bank details to him immediately; thus, allowing him to deposit $1m or maybe I should just interview him for the vacant position of my next ex-husband. I mean he sounds okay, doesn't he? And how would I tell him I'm a one Hugh woman? Whatever nefarious, or honest intent, he had, he's going to find it more problematic now as I have blocked him on any available means of communication. I have no doubt he'll be in some sort of mourning for weeks, or months! He's only human after all.

NSW COVID today has 31 cases. Not good but over 70,000 tests are being done daily. Interestingly QLD imposed a lockdown for just three cases and has eased restrictions despite having five today. Sometimes I have no words. Let me out of this nightmare! Now!

The rest of the day for me was comprised of cleaning, washing, clean bed Saturday and some TV on the horizon. I have red wine too; bought last night when I thought I wanted it but today it's still untouched. So, I have it, but I don't want it. I've just filled up a large sparking mineral water with fresh lime; sometimes you really do get what you need!

Until tomorrow....

Lock-Down-Under - Day 9 - There's always one

Dear diary,

I love where I live. I have a 20-year-old apartment in the trendy Inner South West Sydney. My complex has a lovely pool and a great community spirit, including a Facebook page where all sorts of information is passed. We often see posts on people's Hello Fresh brought inside the complex and placed out of the sun, packages delivered, lifts not working, the establishment of a wee community library... it's awesome.

But then there was one established for this surrounding area of Alexandria too and it's been awesome for seeking and passing information especially when you need plumbers, electricians, nail parlours etc.

But last night was different. It mentioned that there was a little boy missing in Sydney Park.

The Park has been extraordinarily busy during the lockdown, it's a large park with lots of people taking the opportunity to exercise! So many kids and dogs; it's been quite the party park. It would be easy for kids to get lost.

What happened on the Alexandria Facebook page yesterday, restored my faith in humanity. It was almost like a call to arms for people to assist in the search. Within approximately 30 minutes, an extra couple of hundred people, left their homes and joined in. The frightened, lost, little boy was found shortly afterwards, down in an area of the park where there are a few sets of stepping stones over a man-made pond. But there is always one w@nker, this is what he posted!

If they would have stayed home during a lockdown, he wouldn't have been lost....

All spelling and grammar aside, whilst the message he posted is true, it reminded me that it costs nothing to be kind to people. Nothing. Something that escaped him. But maybe he is still only on a day 3 and 4 lockdown attitude with a requirement to avoid sharp implements!

Today has also been a day without Raymundo! Having blocked him on every social media there has been no further contact from him. Sigh. I think I'll miss him.

Alas, there also hasn't any further messages from the hot ex in UK. And I know I'll miss him!

And absolutely nothing from Hugh. Maybe this manifestation process and ideal doesn't produce satisfactory results after all, or for all, or for anybody. Or maybe it's just me it's not working for.

Today is Sunday. Sunday for me is bulk cooking day. Religious, or maybe considered a slave, to my calendar and tasks, another gigantic pot of soup has been created, along with salad preparation, pickled onions and some zucchini fritters! All completed whilst trying to remain engaged on a two hour monthly executive committee meeting. I'm a woman, see me multi-task!

NSW COVID today has only 16 new cases. And 14 are already in isolation! A good indication or process, tracing and maybe honest reporting. Either that, or I am just gullible. Not beyond the realms of possibility.

It's a beautiful day here, what a way to enjoy a weekend! Maybe I'll complete it with a nice gin and tonic, or three.... Whatever the number, I am confident there is alcohol on the horizon. It has been over a week after all! It's the end of day nine.

Lock-Down-Under - Day 10 – every cloud….

Dear diary,

How on earth can I have ten sets of pyjamas in the washing? Lots of sports clothes (mainly used for leisure) and only one "going out" type of top/shirt.

This is an indication of the slippery downhill slope my dear reader; a downhill slope where the indicators show you've spent far, far too much time in PJs. The laughable thing about all this is that it has hardly made a dent in my PJ drawer. I clearly have far too many sets of passion killing nightwear.

Maybe this lockdown should be the time where I have a long hard look at myself and at the hoarding, I have done over the last 25 years – and I know it may even be in excess of 25 years but cut this girl a break on being able to lie about her age in this emotional time. The truth of the matter is that I've never met a bargain I didn't like! Then a clean out is overdue! That's it, a clean out. I have allocated myself a new lockdown task.

And I'll do it, I absolutely will. I've decided. I am resolute. And I'll get straight down to it, right after I've walked to the post office and picked up the parcel I ordered online a few days ago. The irony of it doesn't escape me.

This lockdown, dear reader, is also reminiscent of the (not so) good old days when I was serving in Afghanistan, where for me internet shopping was the sport of the day and a much-needed therapy distraction. Every day, and twice at night in fact. A frequency much like the daily close contact with that sexy UK ex but we will keep that between us. In Afghanistan, access to a US Post Office Box delivery methodology meant Amazon got an absolute flogging and I remember those wonderful days of buying 12 pairs of shoes. I needed every pair, every single pair; including the Ivanka Trump ones that I have placed into a four-year sabbatical, a little out of protest. Today I am forced to admit that I have absolutely no more shoe space left in any of my wardrobes but none of those precious possessions are being cleaned out. Oh no – not the shoes.

But what has been great about this COVID lockdown, social media diary writing, is the contact with all the Australian Jennies Wrens. We may have a reunion. We may have some drinks. We have friends out there we haven't met yet. Silver linings on every cloud.

NSW COVID figures today, 31 cases. How can we have gone back up to 31 cases? How? But at least 28 of those are already in isolation. Let's hope the figures go down so we can be free from captivity and work can resume next week, despite with whatever additional precautions!

Until tomorrow, and maybe a glass or four of whisky by then. If Donny Raymundo hadn't been as sleezy, maybe we could have Zoomed over of those whiskys. But alas, he was slickier than the water around the Exxon Valdez....eek.

Lock-Down-Under - Day 11 – Like holding a lion in captivity

Oh, dear diary,

You know me, I am woman hear me roar on the outside, but with such a placid interior.

However, this morning I am ready to hurt someone with a baseball bat – it's just luck and the fact I don't play baseball that I don't have one handy. I do have the walking stick my father left after his last visit though, which would do the trick and be easier to wield!

It's no-one or nothing in particular. It's just that I don't enjoy working from home. I mean don't get me wrong I love being at home and could spend over a week without realizing that I hadn't left the house. By the time you vacuum, dust, wipe around the bathrooms, have a few cups of coffee and read the news in the morning sunshine, half the day has gone. So, I don't mind being in isolation. What I do mind, dear diary, is bringing the outside work into my girly, penthouse, gin sanctuary. I mean it just isn't right.

And to make it worse, I phoned a friend this morning to complain about it. I like to phone a friend. Why should I keep this displeasure to myself when I can get the monkey off my back and onto a friends? Isn't that what friends are for? I'd happily listen to them. But this morning, no friend to speak to. No answer to my very urgent call. Doesn't she know this is important? What the…? The next thing dear diary, I receive a text. She's unavailable as she's POLE DANCING!

WHO THE HELL POLE DANCES AT 9AM ON A TUESDAY MORNING? I won't mention names here, dear diary, to protect the indulgently, guilty party but I'll just say – Queenslanders! In order to overcome my not-so-surprise at this early morning saucy activity from this particular friend I thought I would do one of the tougher jobs.

I figured now was the time to try and stuff some of those eight pairs of pyjamas into the small drawer they miraculously appeared from and maybe do some cleaning out at the same time. I mean really, do I need those pink PJ shorts with the watermelon design? Or those flannelette leopard print pants that used to hang sexily of my hip bones and now only stay in the same position as that's as far as they'll fit over my arse! I didn't realise that even washing in cold water could shrink garments so significantly!

NSW COVID cases today are only 18 with 16 already in isolation – better scores than yesterday. We may be on the decline with freedom in sight. Only two unknowns on the loose!

Now with only 2 hours of working from home remaining today, I'll console myself with a raspberry and pomegranate tea before a nice little Aperol Spritzer or five.

Until tomorrow, dear diary. Until tomorrow….

Lock-Down-Under - Day 12 - when a small extension is not as sexy as it sounds

Dear diary,

Earlier today the NSW Premier announced an additional week of lock down. I've resisted the red wine until now, but I think this may call for it. And no doubt at work, there will be people happy to have another week at home. But not me, I'm dying to get back out into the wild of Sydney!

Today however, I was fortunate enough to be rostered in at work which was great. Actually, speaking to people and seeing their faces... who would have thought that this simple act would be so precious one day! I even escaped the office for a few minutes and undertook a safety inspection around the site with my Facilities Manager, checking the WHS compliance issues from earlier in the year. And it's amazing what is in these classrooms and staff rooms. Absolutely amazing. Who would have thought there would be so much nice chocolates left over the school holidays.

I asked my Facilities guy, "We still have mice?" He looked at me, looked at the chocolate and responded. "shouldn't leave that around!! Attracts all sorts of rodents!" So, one for you and one for me.... And now here I am, some lovely luxurious chocolate without having to go to the shops! See how this lockdown has affected me; it's turned me to larceny! But I've subsequently discovered that it's World Chocolate Day, so who cares?

I also had to wash hair today. I absolutely cannot believe that the simple act of cleaning has turned into such a significant event, yet here I am! Honest to goodness, I've realised that I've turned into a ponytail or hat wearer during this period. And I haven't even picked up the dry shampoo! Oh diary, how I've changed! I flaunt the conservative personal hygiene standards. I'm a woman on the edge. I tell you, I am. ON. THE. EDGE.

If I get to a day in the same PJs, I'm going to need an intervention!

NSW COVID today has only 29 cases, all already in isolation or connected to a known case. Not great but not horrific.

So tonight, maybe a glass of red wine or five. Remembering those wild days of potential to meet Donny Raymundo! Sigh.

Until   tomorrow.....

Lock-Down-Under - Day 13 - another day release....

Dear diary,

I feel like I'm cheating as I've rostered myself back in at work today again. Oh, the luxury of my pokey, paper ridden (inherited) office, with its three massive screens and the ability to adjust temperature from -2 up to Barbados in less than 5 minutes! Order me that bikini, stat cos I'm a woman with her finger on the temperature up button.

Its winter here in Oz so I welcome heat from any source. But due to this second escape, I am truly as giddy as a schoolgirl getting ready for her first kiss; which from memory was usually accompanied by the obvious clumsy attempt at a left breast grope! Ah, those inexperienced overly ambitious schoolboys.

In fact, it was nearly as exciting as my walk to the shops the night before when I happened upon the tradies just knocking off. It was these guys, who after a long hard day getting sweaty and a little more muscular on a building site were starting to mill around right in front of me. I mean right in front. It was at this point dear diary that I may have let myself down. Maybe if I hadn't been staring quite as hard at Mr Hot Body Builder with his cute shorts and great legs, I wouldn't have tripped over an uneven pavement and given a very loud "oh f*ck!"

Not at all lady-like, dear diary and I am all about trying to be lady like. I really am, but it's been a year in development with limited success if we're being brutally honest. Scottish and an ex-sailor so Tourette's is a gift!

Last night I attempted an impossible feat; to fit those significant quantity of newly cleaned PJs back into the tiny drawer. Yeah, not a hope! I ended up having to pull the entire contents out of the drawer in an attempt to rationalise and maybe, God forbid, throw some stuff away. I am not sure I'll manage to work myself into the level of emotional state that's stable enough to throw things out – but maybe one day.

However, this whole evolution turned out from being emotional into being quite the delight.

The things you find!

One of the surprise things was a saucy little black slinky number; hidden from sight at the bottom of the drawer, waiting for the next ex-husband to appear. I had to blow the cobwebs and dust of it! But I've found it, and the time is right as now there is Don, the wonderful, eloquent, Don Raymundo to consider, never mind hot UK ex. Who, incidentally, still feels it necessary to check in on me.

Oh yes diary, I think I've still got it.

This old girl still has it. Yes siree!

COVID NSW cases today are thirty blooming eight. Thirty-eight. Don't people know not to visit extended families especially when you have an extended family of over 50! Seriously guys. Common sense. However, it's never been very common as evidenced by the man who left Sydney to travel five hours out to Mudgee to meet someone he met on social media. The things we do for a leg over! I mean really.

I think I'll indulge in a sherry or six tonight and enjoy this amazing sunset.

Until tomorrow, dear diary. Unti tomorrow…

Lock-Down-Under – Day 14 – all the fours....

Oh, my dear diary, dear, dear diary.

Have I moved to some other country where the Human Rights legislation is down the gurgler? I mean, what the hell is going on in Australia?

They have deployed the police into Western Sydney to enforce the COVID restrictions. Police enforcement of curfews and movement. Over 100 NSW sworn, armed officers with nothing to do but instructions to check us all. Hang on, be still my beating heart! Hugh who? I hope they have nice arms. I do like a policeman with nice arms. That's not to say that it's a substitute for a man (any man) having his own hair and teeth. Oh no.

But dear diary, why the additional police? I know you're curious about why the Police Commissioner, or Senòr Meek as I like to call him (never to his face but his senior staff think it's hilarious), why Senòr Meek has sent men my way. It's not because he's met me and thinks I'm a firecracker in need of a bloke, nor I suspect has he decided to assist with the search for the next ex-husband, furthermore I do not believe he is concerned that stalker sleaze bag Donny Raymundo is on the loose, oh no! Nope as stated this is to enforce NSW Government Public Health Orders on movement and home visit restrictions. And as I write this daily therapy diary, I pause to wonder what is going on in the world. We are all locked in our homes with police enforcing this lockdown. With no actual end in sight. No end in sight.

As a bit of background about an area I am really passionate about, and cos we should never miss an opportunity to learn something, here is your daily bit of knowledge from Lee's Head of Useless Crap. Western Sydney is an amazing, vibrant community that embodies the statistic of 30% of Australians were born overseas. It has a greater diversity and larger amount of CALD/LOTE families. That's Culturally and Linguistically Diverse or Languages other than English, where the family unit is generally larger, maybe closer and it would seem, certainly more up for get togethers and entertaining. Well, it would appear that all the inter family socialising has increased the transmission of the virus. And to be honest, in my escape days when I venture out to the school site, it almost looks like a celebration out west. The streets are full, cafes are open and busy and not many masks in sight. Hence the numbers are up, and it would appear from the police intervention, so is the Western Sydney freedom, flaunt the rules game!

By how much, I hear you ask dear diary....

Well, NSW COVID cases today are up to 44. Not flash at all.

Also, within the last 24 hours, I had a lucky escape. I was about to duck into IKEA to pick up a lamp. Thankfully because of my "every penny is a prisoner!" attitude, I delayed until next pay. Fortuitously for me it turned out as one of the workers was infected. A bullet dodged by me, only due to my admittedly insane but continual desire to save the first penny I ever earned. Once a Scot, always a Scot.

So again, it looks like I'm in lockdown for the weekend. What to do, dear diary. Well, there's always what's left of that bottle of voddie and more than a little bit chuckling over a post the NSW Police put on their FaceTube page – this is so us right now! I have hit every one of those 'stations' in the last few days.

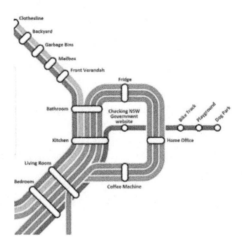

Until tomorrow, dear diary, sigh ....

Lock-Down-Under - Day 15 – it's a slippery slope

Oh, dear diary, for the love of the wee man, I mean really?

This lockdown is affecting me in some very different ways. One of which is turning day into night - and night into day. Rainy days mean no walk and a lovely long ability to sleep in late under a very slumber-inducing 15tog quilt. The consequence of this means I am up all night and not in a good Hugh-like deep and meaningful conversation throughout the night way.

Now that's all very well, but you know it's a bloody horrid night when you are still awake at 3am watching videos on FaceTube. What adds insult to injury? When what you are watching is the world's ten most unique individuals and now you find yourself alone with images of 7ft 8in men in bad suits; it's then when you know it's a really bad, bad night. I seriously felt I was only one small step from watching cats versus cucumbers or Tranny make-up lessons. Then it's game over for sanity and you absolutely know you have entered that warp hole of watching rubbish from which there is no known escape.

Today actually ended up as being a lovely day and I took the time to thank everyone for checking in on me. Girlfriends from Canberra, the US and a lovely ex work colleague whom I haven't seen for a long time. Then there is also the hot UK ex. Man, do I look forward to those messages. It is really greatly appreciated for a hot blonde girl living on her own. Sigh…

It was also a busy day with a whole pile of work matters that required urgent attention so that being now complete it's time for a rum and coke or two. You know the old saying; one is too many, ten is not enough! That might be me tonight; then by God I'll sleep!

COVID NSW today has 50 cases and 29 have been rampant in the community, which effectively means by the whatever amount degrees of separation and subsequent face to face contacts, there is a danger of over 15,000 being infected. Foolish, foolish folks. It was only a week ago that we were at 17 or 18. FFS.

Thankfully I haven't been to any of the sites, in fact I haven't been anywhere at all. I am here. Alone. Here, alone, for another indeterminate number of days. Once again, I reflect back to the effect on people's mental health. What we don't know now that's going to bite us on the arse later. I consider my experiences have made me a little more resilient, but what about people who aren't? especially children.

However, from a necessities (sp intended) perspective, I am stocked up. In fact, I'll run out of toilet paper before I run out of tonic water and that will be about mid next year, so I am good. It's like being a doomsday cult member!

Anyway, until tomorrow dear diary…

Lock-Down-Under - Day 16 - it's a cyber rich crime spree

Oh, dear diary, I've had enough today.

Now before you worry about me and consider that I may be contemplating some self-harm – it's not like that. On waking this morning with the intent to go for a walk, clothes all prepared and some funky shoes at the ready – it was persisting down with rain. So, at 7am, I thought I would catch up on some work, so dragged the work laptop into bed, discarded the idea of a Zoom with hunky hot UK ex and got straight in about it.

Now sometimes you forget that other folks don't rise as early as you do so after sending 2 or 3 texts and about 10 emails, other people started to stir, some complain (oops!) and then respond. Next time I looked at the clock it was 11am, and I was bloomin freezing cos I was still in my lighter night PJs, and to compound it all my back was killing me. Plus, plus dear diary I hadn't had a cup of tea or coffee. So, I went straight to the nuclear. The biggest, fullest bacon butty and a big mug of tea. I was tempted to hit the red wine first but there is that slippery slope again.

The rest of the day has been more of the same. When I started writing my diary it was 4.30 and I was so so ready to turn off my computer for the day. Confirm that this is Sunday dear diary; is it really Sunday?? I mean, give a girl a break. I have so much more I could be doing. But due to COVID and movement restrictions, it would be mainly watching Hugh, NCIS, Hugh, JAG, Hugh or the new season of Virgin River which has just dropped on Netflix.

Maybe this COVID crisis is also bringing out the worst in people though dear diary. A few hours ago, I received a message from a friend asking for a loan of $600, which on questioning her, she didn't know anything about.

Another friend was defrauded $10k by clicking a link he received by text. Now there is a lesson. NEVER CLICK ON LINKS, MUM is something I find myself continually telling her. Thankfully my friends lost $10,000 was eventually recovered, but this is becoming ridiculous, and I think is probably the tip of the iceberg for cyber-crime. Strap yourself in boys and girls, you're in for quite the ride.

Finally, in what seems to have been a cyber-crime extravaganza, I heard on the news today that someone hacked into the NSW Dept of Education; presumably to change their shitty 2020 COVID affected grades.

NSW COVID figures today are 77. Seventy, bloomin, seven – are people stupid? I mean really…? I may be locked in captivity until my tonic runs out and I've worked through all my PJs! I may need to have PJs sent into me (online shopping – oh hooray). A situation similar to the undercrackers I had sent to Iraq when I was deployed there. In that instance, the nasty twin tub washing machine ate about six pairs in one wash. As a bit of background, my husband had helped me pack. Pack light he said. The result being I was nearly running around Iraq with a bare @rse and needed to have underwear sent in to replace the mangled panties. Thank goodness I got rid of the husband! Clearly bad judgement – mine and his.

Okay today is National Mojito Day so I'm off to have one or four. I didn't ever think I would hear myself say that again after one very dodgy mojito in Zanzibar a few years ago, but here I am any port in a storm.

Until tomorrow.....

Lock-Down-Under - Day 17 – the wonderful world of sport

Well, dear diary, what a weekend it's been.

And what a Monday to end the weekend. Australians love sports, they really do. They love, watching, attending, chatting about and betting on sports too. Well, to be honest they love betting on anything; two flies crawling up a wall is at least a Schooner (an Aussie volume of beer between half and one pint). But with Aussie sport, it's not all cheers and smiles. In a statement that will no doubt upset some of my fellow countrymen, Australians lose badly at sport and win with even less grace. Such is the passion here.

So, this weekend you can imagine the delight of this, my adopted, nation to see both Ash Barty and Dillion Allcott win at Wimbledon. Ash Barty is the darling of Australian tennis and she won with sufficient delight to be awesome, and sufficient humility so that Australians wouldn't start on a Tall Poppy extravaganza. I've observed that this is another well participated Australian sport. There have been some significant celebrations over here. Jubilation. Joy. With much living vicariously as a member of her support group. This group is wonderfully named 'the Barty Party'.

I see there may have been some football happening too. Which is why one of my staff was late this morning. Her surname is something akin to Mastrianoni and she came in chanting "It's going Home to Rome!" Whatever that means... but I think it was an England versus Italy game with maybe an Italian victory.

Now for a sport loving nation we tolerate football or more colloquially, soccer but we absolutely love NRL, AFL and Netball. NRL causes the nation to go wild especially during a little competition called State of Origin. A clash of the giants in NSW and QLD causing the populations in both States to don their tribal colours. NSW is fine, it's blue. It's a nice baby blue in fact that compliments my hair and skin.

QLD is a little more complex. Their shirt is burgundy, but it's not called that. It's called maroon, but it's not pronounced like that. It's not maroon as in moon or room, its maroon as in own so effectively mar-own. Of course, Australia does teach English in schools, but I think it's to the same level they taught me in Scotland. Sets a low bench and often fails to achieve it!

But back to sport and AFL. Oh my, oh my AFL; a bunch of muscular, waxed beasts with lots of testosterone, sculpted figures of masculinity in tight shorts and tighter vest tops... oh hello! I like watching AFL. Netball, same same as before, but they wear skirts! Just kidding! I needed to add in the kidding part as I have lots of friends who are huge followers of netball, for some inconceivable reason.

COVID NSW today, well WTAF, it was above the 100 predicted with 112 cases and 46 of whom were again running rampant in the community whilst infected.

There were also 105 police infringements– the infringements included a 15-man poker game in a small apartment in Marrickville. Their ages? 16 and stupid? Oh, no, no, no dear diary. They were between 50 and 90! So clearly old enough to know better. Interestingly, when writing this and telling this tale, I had to refrain from vocalising it as that would have been a sound only dogs could hear. I mean for the love of God, 15 men.

This lockdown may last a long time. I see much alcohol in my future. Work, actually at work, for a few hours today but now in captivity for the rest of the week. Ah well, there's those bottles of Baileys and Butterscotch Schnapps in the fridge that are just taking up space.

Until tomorrow. And how should we pass the night. A few hands of poker anyone…..

Lock-Down-Under - Day 18 – the view from the top

Dear diary,

It wasn't raining this morning, so I dragged my lazy arse out of bed and met a friend for a walk over in Sydney Park. To provide some context or perspective, Sydney Park is about 20 steps from my apartment complex and its beautiful. It's very similar to Central Park in that it's in the middle of the city with great views, lots of bridges, water, flora and is hugely busy… the big difference is that it's about a quarter or maybe even an eighth of the size and not surrounded by $20m apartments.

It was an amazing hour of walking. It was sunrise. There was fresh air. People were smiling. My friend brought me a coffee from a really good coffee shop about a kilometre away. Life was good. And until now, which is ten hours later – that was the last time I had a minute to think.

To say work has been busy today is an understatement. I think I had a cup of coffee about 8.30 but to be honest, I can't blooming remember whether I did or not. I know I haven't had breakfast. I certainly didn't have lunch and stupidly I haven't drunk water all day. My back is killing me, and I have a headache, but I think that's from lack of water combined with far far too much screen time and even more talking.

But the good thing is that two little men came to fix my balcony today – there was some issue with the tiling – and they spent some time getting it all sorted. Despite the fact neither looked like Hugh, I gave them water and made them a coffee as they were here for three hours but somehow forgot about myself. Idiot, yet still exceptionally sexy little blonde.

Where angels fear to tread wasn't my motto today either and I didn't venture to ask which part of the Public Health Order gave them the dispensation to be working in peoples' homes. I mean who looks a gift horse in the mouth? But it's funny being in your own apartment and actively avoiding others who are also in it and putting on a mask when within about 10m. Better safe than sorry. On their departure I found myself disinfecting everything touched or even anything in close proximity that they may have accidently breathed on.

So, statistics for today:

40 phone calls
4 Zoom meetings
154 emails dealt with
23 invoices processed
5 recruitments arranged
1 minor school IT … catastrophe
2 workmen coordinated for 3 hours whilst braless.

The last part I wish I had realised on their arrival not on their departure.

Ah, dear diary, it seems those long destroyed plans of a Page 3 girls' career still haunt you, 30 years later!!

NSW COVID cases today 89 (down from 117) with about 21 rampant in the community and 75% of the cases were family transmissions. What a lovely family gift, a nasty disease! The next few days will tell but they have tightened up restrictions on the worst affected suburb (Fairfield)

Right dear diary, there is a half-bottle of champagne left from last night and an empty stomach, so I may be in bed by 6.30.

Until tomorrow, hic .....

Lock-Down-Under - Day 19 – hero worshipping for beginners

Oh, dear diary,

What a great day.

Today was so much better than yesterday and nowhere near as busy. I fact it's five minutes before finishing time and I am done. Completely done. Ready to sign off with careless abandon, in fact.

Today started with a good walk. Warmer weather always makes it more pleasant in the Australian winter. I managed to get a bit of work done first and eased into it instead of the chaos from yesterday. There are always a few catch up calls to do in order to make sure all my team were alive, well and sober – and a few hours of work. It's been so good. No workmen to entertain braless today. No frantic calls. No missing breakfast and lunch. And I've actually managed to consume water, tea and coffee. It's like a parallel universe. I'm a happy woman! A happy, but locked up, woman.

In fact, this lockdown shit could be a great thing! It really could.

But I think it is time to recognise some of the amazing people making decisions and providing advice on the health and recommendations for lockdown in Australia.

First is Dr Kerry Chant. Kerry is the NSW Chief Health Officer; a woman who was relatively unknown until 15 months ago. She is a woman who, like most, didn't expect that she would have such a hands-on impact in the safety of millions of people during a world-wide pandemic. She is a woman who has had to face the news media every day, a lady who broke the arm of her glasses yesterday, and undaunted, shoved the one-armed specs back on her face, smiled wryly and kept going. She is an absolute champ. A hero. And will be legendary. Insert any girl crush emoji here.

Then there is Brett Sutton who is the Victorian equivalent. He has become an absolute pin up boy over the past 15 months with the hashtags GluttonforSutton or CHOttie trending for months. This guy is a panty dropper. With nearly a million-woman following in a very short space of time, and his Facebook page "Brett Sutton is Hot", the country has seen many tune in to his daily briefings - hoping for their own variation of briefings no doubt. I will admit here that I am among those women, I mean we are only human!

Then there is Commissioner Mick Fuller or Senor Meek as I like to call him. He's the guy sending policeman to enforce lock down in Western Sydney. Not your classically good-looking rooster but something mongrelly attractive about him, or maybe it's just his power and position that's attractive. Or it could just be me in lockdown where all men are starting to look attractive. Where is Donny Raymundo when you need him? And what's happened to my subliminal messaging to bloody Hugh? Where is he when I clearly need some company?

But all this reminds me of a story recounted by an old friend of mine who is a vet. An animal vet not a military vet. She has always maintained that she had never seen an unattractive man. Her rationale is that she spends all day looking at dogs arses! Despite thinking about this a lot, I've never been able to deny this logic. Nor does it get any less amusing with time. It's still funny, well for me at least.

NSW COVID cases today are 97 with 24 running around the community. Now you may think this is still high but it's all relative as the testing is off the scale with six to eight-hour queues in testing centres. So, I guess it's a positive sign – she says reluctantly approaching the third week alone and unafraid. Or just a little afraid.

Okay, it's now well past the time I am scheduled to finish so it's good night from me and time to do that large glass of lime and soda water. May as well do one day of dry July! I am nothing if not a martyr to a soft drink over alcohol. Oh, wait.

Until tomorrow dear diary, a long night with only a soft drink awaits me ....

Lock-Down-Under - Day 20 – it's a gin sort of night

Oh, dear diary,

It's a quandary.

I don't think I have many words left today. I'm not sure I have any words left today.

In fact, I think instead of pouring my locked-up heart out to you, I need to go straight to pouring something out of the liquor cabinet.

Speaking of booze, which I find myself quite focussed on at present, I'm sure Dan Murphy's is spying on me. Over the last few days, I have had nothing but adverts tempting me to buy gin. And as yesterday was pay day, who am I to refuse? Oh, apart from the fact I am in lockdown. Yeah, small matter of being able to freely go out and shop. But its gin. Surely that's classified among the essential groceries. Surely?

My Dan's

Revisit and relish a past pick

Hi Lee

If you loved Tanqueray Rangpur Gin 700mL before, why not give it another go today? Shop your way, and browse the rest of our huge range while you're there!

I was actually going to walk to the shops tonight but that's not going to happen. No bloody way. Gin, Tom Yum soup with dumplings and a few hours of NCIS – yep that's me. Done.

NSW COVID cases today – 67 with 28 spreading the love wildly in the community which isn't a great figure, but we did have 58,000 people tested. On those figures, it doesn't appear bad, but I am really ready to be free.

Short but sweet tonight dear diary, I don't love you any less, I just love rest more!

Until tomorrow, when my mood and my resilience against alcohol may be improved.

Lock-Down-Under - Day 21 – just a walk in the park

Dear diary,

It's a little freaky.

I know there is this scientific evidence that women who live together start to align in cycles, well I think it might be the same with walking. All the women walking in the park each morning are clones. They all come out similarly adorned in black leggings or running tights, black Nike trainers and a black puffer jacket.

What's with those puffer jackets anyway? Jeez… you couldn't get us to be seen dead in one when we were kids whilst today, they seem to be a fashion statement. A very strong fashion statement judging by the nearly 100% participation rate of park walkers wearing them. I say nearly 100% as I am still a hold out on the puffer. How things evolve and how quickly you start to sound like your granny!

But speaking of attire.

I appreciate a good set of leg coverings as much as the next woman and I was delighted to see the NSW Premiers' AusLan signer wearing a jaunty pair of tartan tights the other day. Look dear diary, I say that I was delighted but my joy was short-lived. Short-lived, I say. And no doubt you'll want to know why, dear diary and I get that.

Well tights are a tricky beast, not passionate and never ever very sexy. You won't find that other actor called Hugh on a movie exclaiming "Oh good lord, those are extraordinarily sexy tights Bridget" Nope. Wouldn't happen, ever.

But tights. Tights are the reason we Wrens were thought of as sexy (well one of the many, many reasons we were thought of as sexy), but it wasn't because we wore them. It was because we didn't.

But back to the subject, tights are tricky. When you put them on, unless you are scrupulous in putting your hand down the leg at the outset of what can be a traumatic clothing experience, followed by putting the toe-shaped bit over your feet, and finally, carefully, pulling them up so they feel comfy – you're always in danger of a twist.

The horrific result of a twist can manifest itself in a variety of ways. This includes having the heel area on the top of your foot and suddenly there is a round discoloured patch where your heel was previously on your last wearing or there is a bubble in the material, and it looks like you have a growth. And there is a very likely chance of a combination of both. Making it both lumpy and aesthetically displeasing. Yes, tights are tricky. Very tricky indeed. But you can be forgiven for getting it wrong in the dark or with dark coloured tights or again a combination of both.

What you can't be forgiven for, dear diary, is getting it so spectacularly wrong like this poor lady today. This is when your tights are bloody tartan. The most famous of tartans in fact. A Hunting Stewart tartan is the red one for those who don't know. But the lines of the pattern were bloody twisted 360 degrees around her right leg! I mean seriously. Is this a new fashion, is it some methodology to use up spare tight fabric and ensure your arse isn't eating 20% of it? Furthermore, I cannot believe that nobody told her. Or maybe they did, and she didn't have time to fix them. Had I been her, I'd have been racing for scissors and would have cut those bad boys right off the legs! She could have kept them a pseudo bloomer type knickers to keep her arse warm but there wouldn't have been a helter-skelter on national TV today. I know, I know, I'm a lady with the vocabulary of a well-educated sailor. But, in reality, I actually am.

I'm incredulous dear dairy, I really am. I feel like there's been a bastardisation of tartan today.

And now to add insult to injury, NSW COVID cases today are back up at 97 with no sign of it dropping. 29 cases of idiots in the community and 75% still family transmission. Sigh.

I don't need to go and have a drink tonight dear diary. Nope, Because I started two hours ago! Saturday night out? Just kidding, I am in my jammies and heading to bed very soon.

Until tomorrow....

Lock-Down-Under - Day 22 - oh, what a day... now what a night ahead!

Ah, dear diary,

No....just kidding.

The highlight of my day was buying a new stainless steel, multi-peg, knicker drying thingy from that store that proclaims to us that it's "Good. Different".

The funny thing is that if I hadn't seen this item for sale last night, and being the magpie I am, I absolutely wouldn't have dragged myself out of bed. In fact, I'd have done as I have previously. I'd have foraged for food from the back of the cupboard, fridge and freezer, before finally existing on tinned beetroot and baked beans. I'd put money of the fact that this charming b2 combination is most certainly not going to attract my next ex-husband. Not a chance I'll give you the tip! Maybe I should have reconsidered the strange stalker, Donny Raymundo! I could have eaten beetroot and beans until my heart was content, but to be sure my stomach would be grumbling.

This afternoon was a quick trip to physio. Awesome, a short opportunity for freedom. To prolong this freedom, I was going to walk. There I was, out the house and into the park which is part one of the journey. I was free. It was at this point; I was exposed to the wind. Holy snapping duck shit Batman, that wind was pretty strong and blooming cold. Any stronger and it may have blown my newly cultivated hairy top lip into some semblance of order! Michael Finnigan has nothing on me. God, I hope this lockdown ends soon or my 'hairdresser' is going to need a machete or a whipper snipper machine!

My lovely physio is an ex-archaeologist! So, he's a man that is very used to looking at old bones. He's also from Surrey originally, so we always have a great chat often reminiscing about UK and I love our sessions. Even more now that he is a legal reason to depart the prison that my wonderful penthouse apartment is starting to feel like it's becoming.

So, after a windy walk back that was more weather based than my beetroot and bean diet, I am ready for a big night watching NCIS! Maybe with a nice rum and coke, what could go wrong with that?

NSW COVID today 111 with about 29 in the community... 59 from family contact and 52 unknowns. So tighter restrictions; well apart from supermarkets, bottle shops, post office, pet shops, and a variety of other bloody shops! But sure, you're all to stay home.

Tomorrow is my second injection or first booster to enhance the initial injection. Even a small prick is better than none! No? Okay, maybe not funny but it's another venture out of the prison!

Until tomorrow, dear diary. Until tomorrow....

Lock-Down-Under - Day 23 - decisions, decisions...

Dear diary,

Today was not so much Planes Trains and Automobiles but more like Trains and Shanks Pony. Having become a fan of public transport a few years ago when I moved to the big smoke, I grabbed the mandatory facial coverings and headed out early to walk to one of the train stations a couple of kilometres away. It was an awesome walk on a sunny, if somewhat windy, morning to Green Square. This was a bit of a change for me as Green Square isn't a station I would normally use. At 8am it was deserted. In fact, during my time on the platform, I saw more trains than people. Well done, Sydney Trains. But it gave me pause to consider a career as a train driver. I mean, they are out. They have freedom. How I envy those drivers right now.

I travelled to the mass vaccination centre that's been established at Sydney Olympic Park for what I am calling Freedom Injection Two. I joined the line, and it was moving so smoothly that I kept walking, straight into the facility, through screening and past the woman who shouts, "great to see your smiling face", on into the injection site. I was in and out within 25 minutes, which included preparation, a pee, a prick and a period of observation! Very efficient. And a great loo. I've always loved a good clean toilet.

On the way back I jumped off at Redfern just to mix it up and walked the few kilometres home. I had the whole afternoon to just relax. Cleaning was done yesterday. Shopping was done yesterday. Washing was done on Friday. So, today I'm looking forward to a big day of nothing! TV, that's it. And it seemed appealing. Relaxing with the TV! Yeah, that was short lived dear diary.

Farmer Wants a Wife. A bunch of sturdy, outback blokes and trying to pick from a group of somewhat cosmetically enhanced women with a preference for Botox and blonde hair dye. No judgement, just an observation on compatibility.

Beauty and the Geeks. A bunch of nerdy blokes trying to pick from a group of somewhat cosmetically enhanced women with a preference for Botox and blonde hair dye. No judgement, just an observation on compatibility.

The Batchelor. A stick up-his-arse, weedy little bloke trying to pick from a group of somewhat cosmetically enhanced women with a preference for Botox and blonde hair dye. Need I repeat myself? I should be a TV critic; I think I am missing a trick here.

Okay, dear diary, searching through the streaming apps it is.

And maybe a nap!

Yep, I'm going to need a nap. Because I am overwhelmed with the news. NSW COVID today 105. Who the f*ck knows how many idiots have been running around the community! Again, I know I am a lady with the vocabulary of a well-educated sailor. Who, in reality, once was, but this is getting ridiculous. I need booze!

Until tomorrow, dear diary......

Lock-Down-Under - Day 24 – whatever gets you through the night

Dear diary,

Does the title make todays diary entry sound saucy?

Well maybe it should.

I had a supportive call from a friend last night, and she (who will remain nameless to protect the obscenely guilty) recommended I watch a Netflix show called SexLife – well, to be honest diary I wasn't that interested cos, well, Hugh, NCIS and JAG, and you know… SEAL Team is my weekly treat. But I thought I'd give this recent recommendation a red-hot go.

Well, red-hot go seems to be the correct description for that little show. During my usual sleepless night when sacrifices and prayers to the sleep Gods had failed, I gave in about 4 am. I watched the first episode, then the second, the third episode took the place of my morning walk and at 7.45 (I start work at 8), I finally dragged my exhausted body out of bed! Right… roll on 4pm today as I'll be working to rule and at 4.01, I'll be finding the remote, TV on, feet up and glass of wine in hand. Deal done! That's my day planned and I'm not unhappy about it at all.

But something else made me giggle today. One of my team posted the following in our WhatsApp group chat.

• Never in my wildest dreams have I imagined myself entering a bank, wearing a mask, and asking for money.

• Never thought my hands would one day consume more alcohol than my liver… ever!

• Lock down seems like a Netflix series: just when you think it's over, they release the next season.

• I'm starting to like this mask thing. I went to the supermarket yesterday and two people that I owe money to didn't recognise me.

• Those complaining that we didn't have enough holidays, what now?

• I need to social distance myself from my fridge; I tested positive for excess weight!

• I'm not planning on adding 2020 to my age. I didn't even use it! I don't know about 2021. Does it exist?

• We want to publicly apologise to the year 2019 for all the bad things we said about it.

• To all the ladies who were praying for their husbands to spend more time with them — how are you doing?

• My washing machine only accepts pyjamas these days. I put in a pair of jeans and a message popped up: "Stay Home"

Followed by summary of annual instructions:

2019: Avoid negative people
2020: Avoid positive people
2021: Avoid people because you don't know if they are positive or negative

Can't wait for 2022!!

It did make me smile at how accurate some of these things really are though. But little did we know that 2022 would only be marginally better with still restrictions on travel to many places. But who doesn't love a good margin?

What didn't make me smile as much. NSW COVID cases today were 98, with 20 oblivious luddites running around the community, probably scraping knuckles on the ground as they go. A year ago, I was tolerant with this whole matter. Now? Yeah, not so much now.

I need a wine and a good Netflix series. Oh, and maybe hot UK ex – if someone could have him stripped and scrubbed and packaged over! Thanks in advance.

Until tomorrow dear diary....

Lock-Down-Under - Day 25 – back to 1982

Oh, dear diary,

Another day, another bottle of wine needed.

It's been four hours of Zoom meetings and another six hours tomorrow. Trying to say I am fully interested in these is like Miss World trying to convince you she can deliver World Peace, singlehandedly. Not a hope dear diary. Not a bloody hope.

But today started with the usual walk over the park which was lovely. Now when you get two Scottish women together with a dog called Archie, the conversation tends to revert to the homeland. Often, it's the Janey Goadley videos where she does a voice-over of the Scottish First Minister, Nicola Sturgeons daily briefings. That never gets old "Frank – get the door" always makes me smile. If you haven't seen it, it's worth finding her FaceTube page or simply heading to Google.

Today though we were speaking about the Scottish Football Team and their continual spectacular underperformance in the majority of their matches and the fact that probably the last time they qualified for a World Cup was 1982, in Argentina. For those of you who were around at that time you may recall that there was a song that went with the 1982 qualifying.

Now imagine, dear diary the absolute joy on the faces of the Sydney Park users this morning when two sexy blonde Scottish women started singing "We're on the march with Ally's Army, we're going to the Argentine!" at the top of their voices, in a decidedly off tune, but still delightfully pleasing, manner. I think those were the looks of delight my dear diary, I really do. Pure delight.

But speaking of delight, I must admit I haven't watched any further episodes of SexLife. I am however stunned dear diary at the amount of my friends who have watched it and had paid particular attention to s1 e3, specifically at the 29-minute point. I can't recall what they were talking about so I may need to watch it again. Oh, and maybe again, just to familiarise myself with what all the fuss is about. Yep, there it is, the fuss is about a HUGE willy. Maybe they don't have a hot UK ex to compare it to. Alas…

And whilst we are on the subject of disappointment, NSW COVID cases today was 79 – so a slight improvement. But then the other shoe drops and 29 were loose in the community, running amok and spreading their COVID germs to their beloved families; whilst ensuring we are held in captivity for even longer. Gits.

Until tomorrow dear diary. And for those with a lust to know what the song is, the lyrics for Ally's Tartan Army can be found on Google with a video on YouTube. You're welcome, enjoy!

Lock-Down-Under - Day 26 – the worlds sexiest woman

Dear diary,

Sigh.

It's not warm in my apartment. Look it's not freezing like Canberra or mandatory flannie sheets back-on weather but there is a little nip in the air. Contributing to this is the fact that the bedroom/study I have set up to undertake this working from home shit is on the west side of the apartment so doesn't get sun until about 2pm. This is combined with the fact the only reverse cycle aircon is in the open plan living room/dining room/kitchen. So, to combat all these cold atmospherics, dressing for comfort is the way ahead. As you well know dear diary as a Scot we believe there is no such thing as cold, just bad clothing. Same today, I needed warm, comfort clothes.

Since the purchase, I have long held the belief that I own the worlds sexiest Ugg Boots dear diary. They are black suede, mid-calf with the UGG funky bronze label on the back and a little bit of grey and black fur trimming. They are funky and fabulous. Today I combined them with an Irish Fisherman's sweater which makes me look like, well, an ill-kempt blonde wearing an Irish Fishermen sweater. And it does bear more than a passing resemblance to something a cat has sucked and made a cat nest in it. It's well-loved shall we say, I think that's the best way to describe it. It's not passion inducing at all but it's long, comfortable and very warm; in fact, the delightful blend of man-made fibres is quite perspiration inducing at times.

Today I threw it together with some leggings. I'm not built for Lycra. I'm a whole lot of a woman to love and I suspect an image of me in Lycra causes people to say, "I didn't think Lycra stretched that far…oh, it doesn't." But there I was, looking bloody warm, comfy and fabulous, maybe even resplendent, when the postman called me down to the front gate to pick up a parcel. And to my immense horror to be seen by all the other neighbours picking up their respective parcels. Those poor buggers may be in therapy for years.

But I didn't care. I really didn't dear diary because I'd been sent a present and I knew it had something to do with some male model. My ovaries were starting to jump up and clap at the thought of it. (Well, a single-handed clap as I'm one short) And it was indeed a fabulous present! A semi clad male picture, ingeniously made into a 1000-piece jig-saw puzzle. In face there appears to be a series of Sexy Puzzles, Men in Bed. And each has a message for the recipient.

I've been waiting for you. Come, let's spend the evening together in bed. I'll open a bottle of wine and we can settle in for a long night of pleasure. Start by running your fingers over my tight body. I do so enjoy your touch. Then it will be my turn. We'll take it slow and savor every moment as we indulge in each other's fantasises. We belong together, Bradley.

Oh, hello Bradley, welcome to the Playgirl Penthouse. You and I are going to get down to some fun this weekend. I'm even going to clear and dust my dining table to accommodate laying you flat out over it. Oh yes indeedy! You and me big boy, and some red-hot fun joining our bits together.

I can't wait until the weekend and a big thank you shout out to the lovely Cecilia for thinking of me! When she told me she was sending me something to make me happy, I initially thought "Oh goodie, it's a life size Hugh or even another sort of female toy; I've always wanted one of those!" but this is much better, it'll take days!

But the crappy end of today? Well, NSW COVID cases today were 110 (I mean farking seriously) with 43 screaming raving lunatics running rampant in the community… with one even travelling five hours up to Orange just last week!! WT actual F? I need a gin!

Until tomorrow, dear diary. Until tomorrow….

Lock-Down-Under - Day 27 – what's the story, morning glory?

Oh, dear diary,

What a fun morning and what a sight to behold. No actually, not really.

I think I may actually need counselling. There I was, opening the blind in my study and, there he was, as naked as the day he was born. Stark, bollock naked and posing on his balcony like he was bloody Fabio.

Thank goodness for a well-placed fence railing, that's all I can say. Well, it isn't all I can say but I was a little speechless as this unexpected sight.

Yesterday one of my colleagues informed the team that she saw a whale from her beachfront house window but was too slow to grab her camera to capture the image. Not so much this little blonde heroine. Quick as a Scotswoman trying to get into a bar after Dry July, there I was, phone in hand and already composing today's diary entry in my mind! It was like it was written for me. Sometimes life is a gift.

I then posted my experience (without photo) on our apartment complex Facebook page. I explained what I'd seen. I asked if anyone else had been assaulted with the view, and if anyone knew him so they could advise him that he was spotted. Well and truly spotted, in fact.

Hilariously, I received a few replies asking which apartment and what time, with a tone that suggested they were sad they missed the spectacle however may be looking out the window at that time tomorrow. No, I'm sure I don't live alongside a bunch of stalkers and that they were clearly asking for a friend.

I wonder if I can have the image made into a jigsaw! Maybe Photoshop out the back boobs, thinks Miss Not-So-Perfect still enjoying her Fisherman jumper and Lycra leggings.

But the less amusing side of today. NSW COVID cases today were 124 with 43 participants in One Flew Over the Cuckoo's Nest yet to be captured from running amok in the community! I see a whisky in my immediate future, I really do, dear diary.

Until tomorrow ….

Lock-Down-Under - Day 28 – the straw that broke….

Oh, dear diary,

Maybe this captivity stuff is affecting me more than I thought.

It's not like I am not used to being isolated. I mean as a woman that's always been a default position, certainly in the military. I was always alone or felt alone as I was surrounded by 98% males. I watched a military show last night and they unkindly called us women, squatters. Right, well guys, if you can get a No 2 out from the completely vertical – it includes you too, as now with 'she-wees' there's a no-squat option available, if required!

But dear diary back to the potential effects of isolation, and off the feminist bandwagon.

Today I had a lovely (for me, probably not for him) conversation with a help desk guy at TransLink (the Gold Coast light rail). They owe me $17AUD and have done since April when I bought two cards for my friend Bel and I to flutter around the Goldie, like the beautiful butterflies we are. It's not that I need the $17 but it's the principle of it. They won't refund my money and said the card had been registered to someone else. I found myself in a slightly raised voice saying I BOUGHT IT AND I WANT MY MONEY BACK. YOU HAVE NO RIGHT TO KEEP IT – ITS TH….TH…. THEFT.

When I sat back and took stock of this conversation and my reaction, it was a telling thing about this lockdown. It may be getting to me in some form of a bad way. Or maybe I was just missing the naked balcony man from yesterday. Maybe I am missing the attention of the stalker-ish Donny Raymundo. Or maybe I need to call hot UK ex. Who knows? I'm laughing about it now. It is funny now. But that doesn't take away from the fact that this is money that could go towards putting petrol in my prize possession, Patsy Porsche! Don't be impressed, she's second hand and I sold my soul for her. All for red leather seats.

So, with a gin already in hand from my 3pm Women, Working With Wine meeting with some of my staff, I can tell you todays other sad tale.

NSW COVID cases today were an all-time high of 136. JACKPOT, with a stunning 53 grubs, lower than a badger's arse, running riot in the community.

Until tomorrow dear diary. Until tomorrow…..sigh.

Lock-Down-Under - Day 29 - the risk of ages.....

Dear diary,

Do you think the way you evaluate risk is a sign of age?

I think it may very well be dear diary. I do. My walking companion emailed me yesterday and instead of going to our regular Sydney Park venue, suggested a nature reserve. Somewhere I wasn't familiar with. She assured me it was within 10kms from my place. The 10km number is important dear diary as that the current restriction on being in the vicinity of your home address to do exercise. You are required to remain with 10kms, presumably to contain the idiots that think it would be a nice two hour run up the coast to exercise on a beach in a non-COVID area and potentially infect those locals. But I digress with my chastising of the idiots, dear diary, back to the point of 10kms. Well, I thought about this for a few minutes and contemplated if it really was within 10kms and if I would really be legal.

And then it hit me. What the actual hell am I doing?

Evaluating risk is something I have done my entire life. My whole job as an Air Trafficker was about risk and now, I'm worried about the specifics of 10kms? It is completely ridiculous when you consider the outrageous stuff I have pulled in my time and lived to tell the tale. I laughed when I thought back about the helicopter trip in Baghdad, that was supposed to be within the confinements of the airport boundary and ended up on a firing range in Fallujah, doing a low level flight back down Hell Highway and ending up in Baghdad city with the chaff and flares going bloody berserk and a foreign bloke that shouldn't have been in the helicopter, standing looking handsomely menacing with a long barrelled weapon asking, "who's the Blonde?" Who's the Blonde? Who's the Blonde? WTAF? I mean, dear diary, holy snapping duck shit. The helicopter is lighting up the sky with the electronic self-protection equipment, as its being shot at and that's his only question.

As an aside to that adventure though, was that the scariest part of this was facing my boss when I got back from my one-hour trip, nearly five hours later. "You f*cking won't be doing that again de Winton, will you?

And now 10kms, pffft. 10kms radius zone, I speet in your general direction (imagine French accent there!)

As it turns out, after a thorough check, I was within 10kms, but it took some thinking about. The conclusion to all these thoughts is - I'm getting old, dear diary; old, old, a little older but still like some rules and order.

Now speaking about what is getting old. That is the NSW COVID figures, 163 today with 42 in the community. Yeah, I'm not getting outside 10kms for a while. So, it was lucky that today's protest march was in the Sydney CBD......THEY WILL NEVER TAKE OUR FREEDOM!

Until tomorrow dear diary, until tomorrow......

P.S. No, I didn't take part in the protest. Their behaviour was deplorable. However, we are months and maybe years away from getting out of this mess and in a worse position than we were a year ago. So, we need something, but not this and not violence.

Lock-Down-Under - Day 30 – ♪♪♪♪Sunday Morning, up with the lark…

Dear diary, what a bloody mess.

Who would have thought it could happen to this extent here? Earlier this year the world watched in horror as marches on the US Capitol Building got hugely out of control and you wonder what madness overtook the crowd. Well whatever madness it was dear diary, it found its way here yesterday. Right here in Sydney. Instead of people taking selfies of themselves sitting at the Speakers (of the US House of Representatives) desk and at her podium, we had a bunch of clowns climbing on building canopies and punching horses. Something I didn't think I'd ever see outside a cartoon!

A lifetime in the military, dear diary, a lifetime and it was always highlighted that one of your 'raison d'étre' is to protect democracy; well yesterday makes you wonder if the hard work of thousands of Defence personnel is really worth it; especially if the result is what happened yesterday. Is this really what we are fighting to protect? But I guess it is this week, dear diary, I guess it is. Surely the luxury of living in a democracy is we protect their right to do this, to protest like this, and don't discriminate against the spectacularly stupid. Well, not openly anyway!

But today dawned as another new day and we were greeted with the news that multiple arrests had been made including the git that assaulted the horse. Yeah, I'd like the punishment to fit the crime and it be him tied to the horse, maybe by his ankles and the horse given a quick slap on the arse to make it take-off on a fast run. I know a quick slap on the arse always gets me going!

But another day in lockdown and another adventure for me. Today was a delightful walk around the trendy inner west city and up to the new deli supermarket at South Everleigh. The developers have created this amazing, funky, industrial chic retail precinct in the old railway yards with a lovely display of old equipment, all cleaned up and looking spiffing. The deli is part of it and has one of the best selections of meat and cheeses that I have seen – it actually has its own walk-in cheese room! To further add to the appeal, it's even delightfully named Romeos. Tres, ooh, la, la!

NSW COVID cases today are 141 with 79 running around the community infecting everything they touch and breathe upon. I have no words but it's good job I stocked up on cheese – that'll mean a cut down on loo paper too! Well, for a short time!

So, until tomorrow dear diary, when I promise to cease murdering the French language. I wonder though, how many people reading this actually read those parts in a French accent? And how many of a certain age continued the song from today's title? "Sunday morning, up with the lark, I think I'll take a walk in the park. Hey. Hey. Hey. What a beautiful day!"

Lock-Down-Under - Day 31 – distractions, distractions

Dear diary,

It's been a busy day for me mainly because the powers that be brought my Board meeting forward to 4pm. So not much time for you today my love. It's been all Board (bored) preparation and not much else really.

How spectacularly uninteresting my life is at present. I am currently sitting on two laptops, one with a slave screen which feels like it is only a one stop from the bridge of the Starships Enterprise! Oh, I always wanted to be Lt Tasha Yar. Just a little imagination makes the day go better – Hugh.

I say that my life is uninteresting but that's apart from the Bradley jigsaw. That was pretty interesting dear diary. But probably not in the way you're thinking. I started assembling Bradley this weekend. I'd forgotten how long it's been since I did a jigsaw and how many times you have to go through the box to find the frame pieces, especially when it appears that you have a boy look the first time. I am up to three times searching those pieces and at one point I nearly turned the Bradley jigsaw into Bradley confetti.

I showed hot UK ex the puzzle and the finished image and informed him that I could make a jigsaw out of his picture so I could run hands over him. Typical bloke, dear diary, straight into it, he asked how many pieces I thought I'd need. Ah the arrogance of the male of the species. Less than six, was my response!

But something far less attractive is NSW COVID cases today; 145 cases with 51 running riot in the community. Thank goodness I am not doing dry July, dig in folks this is a long-term lockdown!

Until tomorrow dear diary, once more, sigh……….

Lock-Down-Under - Day 32 – Martial law approaching? Ok well, bring on the Welsh Guards

Oh, dear diary,

I'll start this one with BLUF - Bottom Line Up Front.

NSW COVID cases today are 172 with 60 infectious in the community. I mean, really? Worst day ever, well until tomorrow but the look of the trends and the behaviours of our community!

I'm in a really bad place at the moment. Not mentally, I just live in Sydney.

Many of today's cases are from a party in an apartment. Now consequently, there is a full apartment block in lock down and being guarded around the clock by police. Guarded by police, dear diary, big muscled, officers with even bigger weapons. Oh, be still my beating heart.

At this rate, they'll be calling in the Military and we will see the Australian Defence Force patrolling the streets with long barrelled weapons and face masks. If they do, I'll be putting in a request for the UK forces to be dragooned over here to do the job. I recall seeing a platoon of the Welsh Guards in my youth. This image has been imprinted on my mind since. It was quite the sight. Maybe, just maybe, I'll be called back to action dear diary. It may be a call to arms, and I'll be back in uniform protecting democracy and looking bloody magnificent doing it.

Ah, or maybe not. I gave all that kit back and don't even have a pair of strides to wear. And certainly, none that would fit me. So, I am done. Really, truly done. But note to self, just in case *switch phone off*

At work today we said farewell to a colleague. She has a fancy new role with University of New South Wales, and we wanted to give her as good a send-off as online calls and internet shopping could provide. It was so sweet to see her surprised face when we put on the lovely and very jolly 'farewell' background that our Communications Manager had put together for the occasion. Bless.

I'm about to go and make myself a peppermint tea and perhaps an early bed.

Good night dear diary, until tomorrow.....

Lock-Down-Under - Day 33 – I nominate Hugh Jackman. As if it was ever in doubt

Oh, what a day indeed, dear diary.

What a bloody stinking day.

At 11am this morning the Premier announced that lockdown will be extended past Fri 30 Jul and for another four weeks. This means that my wild, drunken, debaucherously uncivilized weekend in Darwin is now off. As is the weekend on the Goldie, scheduled for two weeks later. That's clipped my wings a little dear diary but think of the money I'll delay spending! Always the Scot where every penny is a prisoner.

But what the Premier also announced was a Mental Health initiative for those of us living alone. We can have, what I took to mean, is conjugal visits! This involved nominating one friend that can come visit, a bubble buddy. And one of my girlfriends read this announcement the same way based on this little message. "We are allowed to nominate a person to visit us, just one and that's our f*ck buddy during lock up!" Well, okay. I'm in.

So, for the love of God, can someone now have Hugh stripped and scrubbed, carb loaded and contactlessly delivered to the Playgirl Penthouse. I may even indulge in some false advertising for his arrival and put on make-up and a push-up bra!

Now for the less exciting news. NSW as the bunch of over-achievers they are, topped the COVID charts today at a whopping 177 cases, with 46 infectious in the community.

I've already sunk the first of many wines this evening, it's gonna be another long month.

Until tomorrow dear diary….

Lock-Down-Under - Day 34 – from the mouths of babes…

Well, dear diary,

Well… would you look at that.

Yesterday I joked about martial law and today the Police Commissioner (or Senor Meek as I like to call him) called for ADF help. And voila, cést ici! I like to throw a bit of franglais in cos I'm tres posh, me!

And speaking of good, I really want to thank all of you who have checked in with me over the last month', Bel, Cecelia, Al, Kaz, G, Tan, Donny Raymundo, Hot UK Ex, the amazing Wrens on the FB page and of course my wonderful mum. You have been amazing with all the calls and jigsaws. And a huge thanks to friends and family back home in the motherland for helping mum through what was a shit week. There were a few midnight phone calls I can tell you.

But with the good dear diary, there is also the bad. NSW COVID cases today were 239 with 70 infected and polluting every b@stard else in the community. Don't expect Christmas Cards or presents from me folks – I'll be in lockdown until 2022. At the time of writing, it seemed a remote possibility but, not quite as funny.

I'm going for wine to cope! Until tomorrow dear diary, bottoms up!

Lock-Down-Under - Day 35 – what to plan, what to plan…

Dear diary,

It's Friday night and I'm considering just turning up at the airport with a bag and passport. Yep, I am thinking of jumping on the first flight with available seats for a magnificent, spontaneous, weekend away, somewhere exotic where they serve drinks with little umbrellas. Somewhere I can wear swimmers and risk the production of crackling if the sun hits my arse.

Yeah, dear diary, just kidding, apart from the fact there are no flights, I don't have the energy. After the week from hell, personally and professionally, along with eating salads and home-made soup, I am going for a pizza. For those of you who think I am about to flagrantly break COVID health orders, no. There is an amazing pizza place in my apartment complex. One big meat lovers (phnaar) and I'll be in a carb coma by 6pm. Sounds like my type of night.

And here is the maybe not so bad, NSW COVID cases today were 170 with 46 infected in the community. This doesn't include the riot participating idiots from last week. Those sweet little treasures are yet to show on the infection scale.

I think I'll just make a nice cup of cocoa and head despondently to bed!

Until tomorrow dear diary, bottoms up!

Lock-Down-Under - Day 36 - What can I do for you Officer?

Dear diary,

Mark me excited today.

Oh, I am really really excited dear diary. Is it a new variety of gin? Is it that I just discovered some more space to store shoes? A delivery of Hugh in his scrubbed glory? Has hot UK ex smuggled his 6'3" frame into Australia and offering unlimited foot rubs again?

No. No. my dear diary. No. No. Better. The police commissioner (Senòr Meek) has sent some of his boys my way. Local talent! There I was, setting off to do my weekly early morning Saturday shop and there they were! Over 20 police cars, and 40 law enforcement officers. Oh, halle-bloody-lujah. So, the car was stopped, I wind down the window and respectfully greet the officer in my normal manner.

"Hey Big Boy, come and get it!"

After a laugh, a shake of the head presumably trying to comprehend what he'd just heard, he attempted to compose himself as he approached the vehicle. "Identification please, and where are you going?"

At this point, I decided to play it straight. "I live in the building behind me and am heading to Marrickville for a quick weekly shop!" He handed me back my phone, as I have my license electronically and I saw the chance so took it!

"Hey, whilst we're here. I'm looking for a bubble buddy. Any of the guys here single and could handle a hot blonde with a flash car and a penthouse apartment?" At this point I thought he was going to swallow his mask as the guffaws got louder and the mask movement could have induced a seven on any Richter Scale.

"I'll ask around for you, love. Best I can do!" Fair enough!

Another surprise highlight? This lockdown is great for parking at the shopping centre. I have never seen it so empty! Absent is the need to park 300m away so no git bangs your door! I looked back whilst walking into the shopping centre and I realised my parking is simply awful. It looked like I abandoned a stolen vehicle!

That's the good part of this morning, the not so good. NSW COVID cases are back over 200 and I have no idea how many are in the community! I'm losing the ability to care! But did I say how easy it was to get a parking space? And then there's a potential police buddy.

Until tomorrow dear diary, a little red wine tonight, I think!

Lock-Down-Under - Day 37 – how good is (a) grinder?

Oh, dear diary,

I was spoilt over the Christmas and New Year just gone. I went to stay with some friends and was treated to not only home-made bread but also freshly home roasted and ground coffee beans. It was bliss and I felt I needed an equivalent. So, after my unparalleled fresh coffee experience, I came home and bought myself a coffee grinder along with a supply of some amazing coffee beans. The current ones I have are with a hint of blackberry and chocolate but hadn't been ground. I was about to remedy that little failing. They are divine. It's been a wee while since I'd indulged in fresh coffee, as I've become addicted to different flavoured tea with ginger and lemon being the preference. But today, dear diary, after a disturbed night sleep (just cos), I thought a coffee would get me through today a little more smoothly.

Ah yes, there I was, beans freshly ground, full cafetière, no milk and I consumed the lot. Quickly. Those smooth coffee, chocolate, berry favours were like nectar especially after so long away from the caffeine drug.

Well, it's nine hours later, dear diary, and this is the first of me stopping long enough to sit and write. The list of undertakings has been so extensive, it would probably break Facebook. In fact, dear diary, I am hoping that by 8 or 9pm, I'll be able to peel myself off the ceiling in time for bed. Either that or I am going to need to scavenger hunt for some sleeping pills and be strapped to the bed like Gulliver on the beach in Lilliput.

I have even done my census, which isn't due for another three weeks and was tempted to have some fun with one question regarding language. When they speak about a language other than English, is Drunken Sailor with Tourette allowed? Cos, if it is dear diary, then I am so bi-lingual!

Speaking of things that want to make you say f*ck. NSW COVID figures today are 239 with 46 infectious in the community. Not great but it could be a lot worse. Probably best I start on-line Christmas shopping.

Well, dear diary, I think I have an open bottle of red wine somewhere, so until tomorrow…..

Lock-Down-Under - Day 38 – Meek and Meeker?

Oh, dear diary,

Be still my beating heart.

Not only is it senior police bloke Senòr Meek on the TV, but it's also now accompanied by senior Army bloke Senòr Meek too. Two prime specimens of delicious Sydney male flesh! There they were, on TV, looking all authoritative, commanding and very much in charge, the latter with the traditional old knife hand gesture that is so common to, well actually, all army officers. Oh, good lord, it nearly made my ovaries jump up and clap, dear diary, it really did. I do adore a commanding figure in uniform. Not Flying Suits though, as those things stink.

But my excitement wasn't just because I was looking at some amazing men on TV, oh no. It goes further than that today – I went to work! And I don't mean work in the room next door doing a walk past of the McKitchen for a McCoffee and dragging my sorry arse back the 20m into the study, nope, not today.

Today was freedom!

Today was getting that self-same arse into the car and speeding off down the motorway (with $12.50 toll charges each way!) to my actual physical workplace. Now, before all you jobsworth folks tell me I can't do that, I will direct you to the NSW Public Health Orders and I'll show you where I can. Education. I work in a school with approx. 1000 students and the announcement last week of Year 12s coming into school to do their trial HSC, means that my team of Facilities, Finance, Admin, Cleaning, IT and Bus Drivers need to ramp back up. We need to get the school ready and adjust our COVID Safe plans to do this. There I was, looking at freedom squarely in the face with a glint in my eye and a grin on my face.

But, but my excitement had a second reason. A school with 12 buildings has industrial carpet cleaning equipment and I have some carpets that are in dire need of industrial cleaning. I've been preparing to do this for a while and well before the last six weeks of lockdown. The carpets were even ready to get out as they were sitting on a trolley, in my hallway, waiting. In fact, they have become a feature that I've begun to dust and vacuum around!

Today was the day.

By 7am, I was in the school hall, cleaning! I had to sneak around my cleaners. This was not because I was using their equipment; no, they knew. No, I had to avoid them as they wanted to help. Now don't get me wrong dear diary, I don't mind watching men working and cleaning my stuff, especially ex-husbands, but no way was I allowing my staff to do it. I couldn't imagine facing my mother, the Oatmeal Savage, again if I had let this happen.

I can hear it from here "WHAT THE HELL DO YOU MEAN YOU LET SOMEONE CLEAN YOUR CARPETS? LEE!! THEIR JOB IS NOT TO DO YOUR CARPET CLEANING"

It may be that I couldn't physically hear it as it would have been delivered in a pitch only audible by dogs, but you get the picture dear diary. In my family, we clean our own mess. And they were a mess to be sure.

Other messy things that make you want to say f*ck, NSW COVID cases today are 206, but that is from 117,000 tests. The numbers are staying steady but still high and whilst it's not great news, it's not horrific. But maybe we aren't seeing the results from the protest nine days ago, or maybe we are just becoming acclimatised to these higher figures. I don't know but I do care, despite the fact I got a day release today.

Anyway, dear diary, I can hear a noise in the background, and I think it's a red wine calling. Until tomorrow….

Lock-Down-Under - Day 39 – dirty b1tch

Oh, dear diary,

My joy was very short-lived, so it was.

Whilst the hard work of carpet cleaning yesterday was successful, it was only to a limited degree. The lovely, but somewhat old, Persian-type and look carpets that I have owned for 30 years needed a little more love. Well, let's be bloody honest, dear diary, they needed a lot more love. The industrial cleaner didn't make the difference I wanted and needed. It did brighten them, and the colours were a little more pronounced but not enough. What to do….?? After taking advice from both my staff and the Oatmeal Savage, a decision was made. I would give them a bath.

It was a little like a Goldilocks operation dear diary, not too hot, not too cold, not too much NapiSan and ensure it's all dissolved before putting the rugs into it. That all sounded great in theory. In fact, it was a great plan, well scoped and ready to execute.

And that's where the wheels fell off dear diary.

Looking back on it now, I should have realised, I'm a smart girl, how did this miss me? As I was into hour four of cleaning these two rugs in the bath, I emptied the disgraceful coloured water for the seventh time, lest the colour stain the carpets even more. I cast my mind back over the 30-year lifespan that these rugs had enjoyed with me. I thought of the journey from UK, the 10 plus homes on who's floors they had adorned, the storage they enjoyed between homes, the high traffic areas where they had looked nice, the shoes that had trodden on them in those high traffic areas and finally the four 40kg dogs that used to love laying on them, every-bloody-day for about five years. I thought about all of this, as 10pm came and went and I was no closer to finishing.

By 6am this morning, I was back up to my elbows in somewhat less mucky water and using both a scrubbing brush and shower scraper. The latter which all my friends can assure you, I have plenty. Back at it to clean and scrape out the dirty water.

Lessons:
Carpets are like dogs, hard to clean but need it often
Make ex-husbands clean carpets more regularly
Buy a specific throw-away dog rug if you have more dogs.
Remove your precious, much loved old watch before getting up to your elbows in dirty water!

Other things a little mucky today is the NSW COVID cases are 199 from 104,000 tests but unfortunately with a high number (50) in the community whilst infectious. *shakes head*

I'm now back to work having watched the press conference with the mucky news, and maybe a check of the carpets that are happily drying in the sun.

Until tomorrow dear diary, until tomorrow…

Lock-Down-Under - Day 40 – what's the story morning glory….

Dear diary,

Some of the people reading this will think I've managed to secure a bubble buddy. But they'd be wrong dear diary, as I am not that lucky.

Also, I don't use the term 'secure' lightly… because for me the likelihood is that I would almost have to capture my buddy and keep them held in captivity right now, especially with all the beauty salons closed and the fridge being the only thing that's really accessible. It's a sore and sorry sight right now. But hypothetically if I were successful with the capture and keep, then you'd certainly hear some screaming afterwards. I tell you, dear diary, oh, yes indeed. However, I am not sure how long that situation could be maintained, and I would be able to actually hold my 'buddy' in captivity. Especially when the words being screamed are "HELP! LET ME OUT!!"

I digress, dear diary. The glory of this morning was a walk across the road in Sydney Park again. This has been an absolute treasure for me. My lovely Scottish friend Sherron and her beautiful but somewhat nutty dog Archie are there every morning and it's just a treat. I also love the little café in the middle of the park with its repurposed bin, solar speaker/radio, it's just a happy place. The fact it's busy enough to probably require its own QR code is an entirely different matter. And after my 8km walk this morning, I am far too tired to climb on my soap box regarding this matter.

What I will climb on the soap box for though is NSW COVID cases; today new cases were 233 from 104,000+ tests but now over 100 cases infectious in the community. Really? I mean really. With approximately six Bunnings sites added to the 'areas of concern' list. WTAF? I cannot help but shake my head at this stupidity. I know I am becoming increasingly frustrated, but this is what this missive is about. It's my therapy and release. By heavens do I need it right now.

But you know, at the end of the day, what do I care? I used my lunch time today to go to Poor Toms Gin Shop in Marrickville. They have a sale of mixed negroni spritzers, in a tin! Scream. The Martinny equivalent. Oh, roll on 5pm dear diary, when you will hear the pop of that first tin. Then 5.05pm, there goes the second, I'm a class act. Only stopping short at wine in a box.

Until tomorrow, dear diary…. Hic.

Lock-Down-Under - Day 41 – the great escape … well for an hour or so…

Oh, for the love of God, dear diary,

This COVID nonsense is just darn inconvenient now, so it is.

Staff leaving work haven't been able to return IT so now we're short of computers and have laptops everywhere from Sydenham to Port Macquarie. So today is judgement day dear diary. Today is the 'light a fire under the ass of IT and get our shit back!' Part of the plan involved another teacher, putting our trust in Australia Post, maybe hoping they give us a Cartier watch or a $1m salary or bonus as part of the deal, and also me! I had conceived the plan; written the plan and I was part of the plan. This was a temporary escape, and I was both the instigator and the willing accomplice.

At 7am this morning, I set the plan in action to do a contactless pick up/drive past of one of our former staff and I was heading for a drive. I was heading south, south, south of the city. After checking the Health Orders for essential workers, yep Education is still there, I was off in the car, coffee in hand, navigation system set and a face-full of grim determination to have fun. Again, THEY WILL NEVER TAKE OUR FREEDOM.

Three hours round trip and a couple of wrong turns later I was back home and back into the gulags of sitting in front of the computer playing catch up, having tasted that glorious little bit of fresh air and freedom. I even got home in time to listen to today's bad news….

COVID NSW cases today are 262 and over 100 infectious in the community with five deaths overnight. This is awful, it really is. All just because we don't like not sharing, the Hunter Region has been granted some cases and they go into lockdown for a week from 5pm tonight. This all originated from a beach party last Friday Night. I hope they enjoyed the party as it'll be the last for a while.

I'm glad I picked up those Negronis yesterday.

Dear diary… until tomorrow. Sigh, yep until tomorrow.

Lock-Down-Under - Day 42 – oh dear God, she's really a blonde

Well, dear diary,

What was the phrase? Out of the mouth of babes?

Or was it something to do with only drunks and idiots telling the truth? Well, if it's either of those or a combination of the two, then there must have been some drunken infants on my morning Zoom call.

Last year in COVID Lockdown One, as opposed to COVID Lockdown Two–the revenge attack, one of my friends openly quoted that sometimes she missed having her daily shower. She prepared to start work by simply climbing into leisure wear, turn on the computer and started work online. I poo, poo'd it at the time, dear diary, I really did.

But now I had this in mind, and combined this Lockdown One theory of supposed efficiency and paired it with advice from another friend. She maintained that your hair will be in much better condition if only washed once a week. It needs to be trained to get into this routine and that takes a month. Well, it appears I may have been going a little too long between hair washes. It was probably my hair screaming to be cleaned that saw me picking up the Fudge blue shampoo and Aussie 3-minute-miracle conditioner this morning. The latter ironically you can't buy in Australia. The combination of these amazing luxurious products was delicious. I swear my hair screamed with joy. I could feel its excitement at not being hit with something akin to canned snow. In fact, the hair was so ecstatic, I think it was the closest either of us had gotten to orgasmic this side of the millennium.

This was combined with reinforcement from my morning meeting when an excited utterance came through the computer.
"Oh, Lee have you dyed your hair, it looks lovely and blonde!"

Very rapidly followed by one of my other (male) staff saying…
"Nah, she's just washed and dried it!"

I couldn't do anything but laugh, as they were correct. What's normally in a dry shampoo covered ponytail, was today freshly done as a treat to start the weekend. It felt great but it was also some good feedback. The camera appears not to lie.

Talking of extreme highs and lows, NSW COVID cases today 291. Two Hundred and Bloody Ninety-One. Just short of three hundred. Oh ffs.

Okay, its past my finish time by a long way and I have some red wine open. Oh, and Negroni Spritz in the fridge.

Until tomorrow dear diary, until tomorrow……

Lock-Down-Under - Day 43 - a bloody 5* Michelin Chef, that's me

Oh, dear diary,

This old lock down thing really does make you want comfort food. Whilst regularly I'd avoid chocolate and various other types of food, right now I am craving them.

My speciality in the kitchen is "something runny with pasta", always has been! Well, dear diary, for the last few weeks I've resurrected that culinary skill and have been bulk cooking stuff that looks aesthetically disgraceful but tastes so bloody good. And it comes with the added benefit of being easy to portion up and freeze.

Chilli con Carne and Corned Beef Hash are this week's specials. Neither have the appearance of meals that can be served to a guest but always cause a lovely tummy rub from me. Thinking about it, it may not be an appreciation tummy rub, it could be gas caused by the excessive use of onions, but I don't care. It's warm, runny, delicious comfort food as the end of winter wields its way out.

I'd also like to complain dear diary, as whoever decided a Liquor Store is more essential than a Hair Salon is obviously a bald-headed alcoholic.

I was considering trying to get my beautician to be my bubble buddy, but no joy! She may be rejoicing at this now but she's also the one who gets to pick up the pieces when we finally escape. It'll be a tough, maybe dirty job, but someone will have to do it! Poor Lily...

And in the spirit of soul-destroying tasks, another incredible feat of ridiculous today is the NSW COVID cases today, a stunningly spectacular 319 with over 50 infectious in the community. You've got to be shitting me. Victoria has 19 cases too. Again, I have no words. Christmas here we come!

Ah well, here's to a Negroni, I have a few remaining in the fridge from Wednesday's purchase.

Sigh, until tomorrow dear diary.....until tomorrow!

Lock-Down-Under - Day 44 – Mr Willis of Ohio – "the problems we face in the new century will be far beyond the wisdom of Solomon"

Oh, dear diary,

Those that know will know I am a fan of a 1996-2003 series called The West Wing. Its exquisitely written, subtle, busy and beyond its years. I love it. It's the only program/film that I have watched over and over again. Since 2004, I would say I've watched the series over ten times, and on every viewing I always see something I've missed previously. You may know the reason behind this dear diary but let me tell you again why. When my husband and I split at the end of 2006, I was generally always alone for Christmas, and it always felt a little sad. Having said that, I was never alone alone, as I was always welcomed by my amazing friends over the years. Whilst it's always been wonderful to enjoy the hospitality of my friends, I didn't have family here. Always a little sad.

The West Wing was my way of filling in those 'sadder' times, and they were sad, with something that was an absolute and complete distraction. It was a great way to achieve it. I mean, seven seasons of 24 episodes at 45 minutes each one, it certainly is a lot of distraction. Since my parents retired about eight years ago, they have been here more regularly for Christmas, and it has been a joy. Each year I both rejoice and fear the coming of the Oatmeal Savage. I am always just glad she's on an aeroplane and not opting to come by broomstick! Maybe it's cos dad won't fit on the pillion! Kidding Patsy, I love you guys and you know I always save the cleaning for you! Now, due to COVID and the associated travel restrictions, the complete halt in aviation and lots of people without jobs; including the jobs I was progressing when I left my last role; things have changed – dramatically. Things have changed for people worldwide.

This weekend for many reasons, I started watching my favourite series again. Maybe it was just this particular evening, maybe lock-down boredom, maybe I hadn't needed it at Christmas, but it's now mid-year 2021 and I do. I don't know why exactly but I went searching in the cupboard for the DVD set. Coincidentally in Season One there is an episode (e6) about the Census requirement in the US. West Wing, s1e6 considered the problems we will face in the future. Geez, if it was a wide swing guess back in 1996, they absolutely nailed it.

For those not in Australia, our four-yearly census was on Friday 6 August, so two days ago. However, it brought to mind some of the same questions that were discussed in this episode. How do we count the homeless? How do we count people who have entered our country illegally? And more importantly, as we've seen with COVID, how do we get this messaging through to the CALD/LOTE community? CALD being Culturally and Linguistically Diverse, LOTE is Languages other Than English as previously mentioned.

The NSW Chief Commissioner of Police, Senor Meek (again be still my beating heart) has just released COVID messages in the variety of more common languages spoken in

Western Sydney. Liverpool LGA alone has about 160 languages spoken. Where do we start dear diary, in getting into communities so tightly knit that the intra-family transmission is huge. Senor Meek's message goes to that effort in some way. Engaging with the senior community and religious leaders is another. I feel like we are eight weeks behind on this initiative but then again, I'm not running the country or the State and there's lots of good reasons for that, dear diary. Mainly as it would impede on my social life (but not right at this minute). One has to wonder though, had we commenced this initiative over two months ago, maybe our spread prevention would have been more successful.

Changing to a much lighter note, allow me to reflect on those amazing friends of mine, because they deserve a mention. In the last week, no less than ten friends have called me to check-in: with the same number, if not more, messaging. Dear diary, if we judge ourselves by our friends, then I am very blessed. But it's not only this week, it's those same friends who have opened their houses and hearts to me on each of those holidays and Christmases that I was spending alone. I adore them so much and am grateful for their consideration.

And…And…. And…a HUGE thank you to Bridget for the amazing gift pack that I received on Friday. It was bloody magnificent! Chocolate. Shortbread. Herbal Tea. Organic English Breakfast. And some 'cup of tea' reading material. What a way to spend a weekend!

NSW COVID cases today? No idea. I am writing this at 9am, drinking coffee in bed and watching the West Wing, so the daily numbers haven't been announced yet. I am guessing about 344, but that's the optimist in me!

Today, after breakfast, probably in bed watching a couple more episodes, I'll be taking a lovely walk to pick up some shopping. It's a little rainy but skin is waterproof and fresh air will be a great addition to my day!

Until tomorrow, dear diary as right now I see a bacon sandwich and a cup of tea in my immediate future, so until tomorrow….

P.S. NSW, 262 cases today with 50 infectious in the community!

Lock-Down-Under - Day 45 – when the squirty thing in the loo hits you in the face

Oh, dear diary,

It was going to be a lovely day of escape.

Work that needed a Starship Enterprise of computer screens really needed me to head into the office. Ah, education as an essential working environment is a sanity saver. My office with its two 19" monitors and the laptop as the slave space; it's just delicious. Maybe my fetish for a good, big, screen is because of this lockdown and me not seeing any good, big anything else. I don't know.

But dear diary, I'd forgotten how much I was allergic to this school especially with its semi-automatic air freshener in the loo. I think its sensor activated and I sensor-ed that thing right off the planet when I reached over to close the window for the night, and I got a mouth full of f*ckin sandalwood and bloody vanilla. It may be okay in a gin aroma, but this mouthful was not my idea of evening fun. Maybe at one time a mouthful of pure alcohol would be fun, but those were the bad old days!

Neither was my idea of fun, the six hours I put into completing the school census. Did I say completing? Completing? Right well we could say completing if 30% input could be called complete. The rest has completely vanished, poof, gone. When the system crashed, and I lost two hours of work. That appears to be the way the system reacts when over 3000 schools are trying the same old trick of completing this mandatory reporting for next year's Government grants! I mean it's not as if its critical to the school operation or anything like that. No.

Having been strapped to a desk all day, my back is sore, my arse is sore, my head is sore, my eyes are nipping and my temper is ready to overflow. No, not overflow like my cup is full of wine and ready to overflow, more along the lines of an Icelandic volcano. Why? Why I hear you ask, dear diary. Well, let me tell you.

Not just the work I lost and how tired I was trying to undertake it initially then recover the missing inputs, no, the NSW COVID cases today were 283 with 64 infectious in the community. I mean f*cking seriously? Seriously? ARE YOU NOT LISTENING PEOPLE?

This situation is now resembling one of my favourite jokes.
What do you tell a man with two black eyes?
Nothing. You've already told him twice.

Okay, this is the last thing I am doing on my computer tonight. Home time for a nice lime and soda water, followed by half a bottle of red wine.

Until tomorrow, dear diary, until tomorrow…..

Lock-Down-Under - Day 46 – things that make you go, ooohhh and urgghhhh

Oh, dear diary,

Now don't get excited as this isn't a post about how Hugh turned up in a package on my doorstep nor has the hot UK ex found his way over, although it really could be either with that title. Note to self, I must give that good looking creature a call. The latter, not Hugh as he's not available but if wishing made it so. No, this is about the little things that provide joy and some other stuff that make you want to poke your eyes out with some of the same items that bring you such joy.

The good things and the little things that I adore.
Hot UK ex
Family
Friends
Gin
Wine
Today, six years ago, I was planning on how to transport two giraffes to Singapore
And today, a fabulous $8 cutlery set from Aldi. I love Good/Different.

Some of the, oh f*rk no, things. The creature that pitched up at my office door this morning. Clearly a lack of personnel in the buildings is like an open invitation for beasts to find a way in and cosy up in the cooler August weather. With four legs and a tail, it moved bloody quickly with a screaming blond chasing it.

And, and, and NSW COVID cases today are 356 with up to 100 infectious in the community. I've joked before that we will be here until Christmas – yeah, it aint no joke, no more.

What is even scarier, is the frenzy of lockdown and the mob mentality. Both in Nelson Bay and Ballina, news reports have it that there has been fighting over the meat counters. Serious, honest to goodness fisticuffs. The proverbial windmill of bones. Why? I don't understand. We can still shop. There isn't a shortage of food. We should still be able to be reasonable, but that doesn't appear to be the case. Life is sometimes disappointing, or more accurately; more disappointing.

Anyway, I have a cup of herbal tea in front of me and about five hours of school census data entry ahead. The lovely thing is that my staff, hearing of yesterday's system disaster, have been kind enough to leave me in peace today to complete the inputs. I cannot wait for that gin and tonic later.

Cheers! Until tomorrow…

Lock-Down-Under - Day 47 – round again class leader!

Ah dear diary,

Some of my old military friends will remember that phrase.

It was the words that the drill instructors (gunnery staff) would shout at us when we had screwed the pooch on the 'march past', when practising for a parade. When formed up in a platoon, and marching past the dais where the senior officer would take the salute, if you could keep your lines straight, awesome. If you couldn't keep the lines or dressing straight then you were sent around the parade ground to do it again with embarrassing and loud words ringing in your ears – round again, Class Leader. Three times was the maximum that any class/formation I was part of was sent back around to try it again. Considering the dais was halfway down one side of the square, it was a pretty long way to continually march around and bloody time consuming. But we were never alone. There was always a rag-tag bunch of matelots that were doing it in an even more deplorable fashion that we were. God love sailors. If only hot UK ex was a sailor, he'd be perfect but alas no, just Army and Air Force. It was as if I was being tortured!

But I digress, dear diary. How quickly one gets off track when sailors come to mind! No, todays 'round again' is all about a repeat visit to Poor Tom's Gin paradise. Today was my lunchtime, 30-minute escape to pick up another four pack of Negroni Spritzers and to have a chin wag with the delightful Mel. A friend from a previous job.

This is our second Wed lunch drive past meeting, and we've decided next week will be 4.30 or 5.pm so we can actually have a drink there. We don't care if it's in the car, or sitting on the bonnet, presumably as the bar area is closed. We can just stand on the pavement and sink a tinnie, like the class act babes we are!

What's not a class act is the NSW COVID cases today are 344. Yep, I am done. We are royally rooted! Hunter Region have 16 and 20 in Victoria.

However, did I mention I bought a four-pack of Negroni today. I may be singing by 6pm, God help the neighbours, dear diary.

Until tomorrow…..hic….

Lock-Down-Under - Day 48 – looking out a dirty old window….

Ah, dear diary,

I guess it's the small things right now as today, I seem to be window worshipping. I'll just lay it out there; what a difference a window makes. And I don't mean the one I looked out and saw horrid dancing naked man a few weeks ago, I mean the one in my bedroom that stops the noise coming in. Now that may sound like a stupid statement dear diary, but it isn't.

It's not common to have double glazing in Australia but the bright spark, who owned my apartment before I did, installed a second layer of glazing inside the old traditional windows, in all the bedrooms. Not only does it make my bedrooms look nicer than the existing green metal frames but living in the middle of Sydney, it cuts down the noise significantly. However, last night I forgot to close it. The difference in noise was incredible and so disturbing to what should have been a calm night sleep; it was amazing. Suffice to say, I slept rather poorly and woke late feeling weary. It had nothing at all to do with the extra glass of red wine last night. Nope nothing at all to do with the wine, dear diary. There must be a significant tolerance for that by now.

It's also been interesting to watch todays 'scores' on COVID. Today, the NSW Government had one of the States senior mental health experts talking about people's reactions to this lockdown. It was always something I was worried about and why I started this diary, but now this is very much something I am starting to see at work. It's interesting to see how people are less patient and very much less tolerant alongside sweating exceptionally small stuff. There have been a few occasions this week that I have just picked up the phone and asked, "are you okay?" This is only the staff; I'd hate to image the longer-term implications for students. These amazing sub-adults being deprived of the youthful pleasures and solid peer influences that will make them the adults of the future.

Dear diary, I'd like to say though that I am absolutely fine. This may be a weird time and I know being locked down in home for nearly seven weeks now will affect some folks, but I am okay. I would like to get out walking more, but the last two weeks have been busy, and the walking is about to recommence tomorrow. It would have started today but there was that open window thing, resulting in a weary woman episode happening.

What is very much not fine though dear diary. NSW COVID cases today - 345 albeit from 155,000 tests. But on a slightly more positive note, there have been 9.6m injections thus far, with over 3.4m in Sydney, and a potential for freedom at 70% which is forecast to be by the end of August. At which stage the goal posts will inevitably change again.

Until tomorrow dear diary, until tomorrow…. *Gets up to close the window*

Lock-Down-Under - Day 49 – that's not an ornament now, it's a good-looking gin glass

Oh, dear diary,

Such a development. Today a picture on Amazon didn't prompt me to instantaneously go in hard on internet shopping as it once would have, oh no dear diary, not this time. It prompted me to have a look at what I have around me, as there is always something in my little treasure trove of Playgirl Penthouse.

Today I saw these gin 'bowls' and it took me back to remembering that I had owned some large glasses and that I had disposed of them a few years ago. I figured I didn't need them anymore. I mean what single woman really needs wine glasses that hold a whole bottle of wine in each one? Nah, those days are over, so off they went. However, two years later and the idea of putting gin in them is another matter and very appealing.

Alas but those wine glasses are well and truly disposed of, however there are some very fine ornaments shaped like a large fishbowl that would do very nicely. Look, at the minute they hold pretty stones, crystals and some curled black caterpillar things, that I clearly found aesthetically pleasing at some stage (which have now reached their end-of-life in my home) but they're an easy recycle. A quick wash and I could have a whole weekends worth of gin in there before 2pm! With a refill considered by 6pm, at the latest!

Oh, dear diary. This type of glass, and drink, takes me back to a very pleasurable trip to Las Vegas in 2004. A month on exercise at Nellis Air Force Base, living in the Luxor Casino. My life was hell! What else do you do on weekends but visit every funky bar in Vegas, including the Voodoo Lounge with its signature Witch Doctor Cocktail. Costing the princely sum of $24USD for about ten shots of alcohol, topped up with various types of soda and sufficient sugar to keep you going all night. Then for effect and entertainment, throw in a couple of chunks of dry ice to get that tres chic, smoky effect.

Oh, dear God, how I wish I could remember those days and nights. And if I could also get that red lace bra back from the 'bra rack' in Coyote Ugly – that would be good too!

What may be memorable for more time to come is actually not the NSW COVID cases today, which is a mighty 390 with 60+ infectious in the community. I feel these disappointing numbers won't be the chart-topping news today. No, surely the news that will rock the world today is that Brittany Spears' father has stepped down as her conservator! Poor love that he is, he'll be on the breadline now without the reoccurring millions of dollars of her income and will have to exist on the few million he's allegedly already squirrelled away. How the hell will he cope? Stop the presses!

Anway dear diary, I have a glass ornament to clean in an-ti-ci-pation. Until tomorrow.

Lock-Down-Under - Day 50 – why bother?

No, no, no, dear diary,

I am not addressing the NSW COVID cases of 466 today. I am not asking why the hell are we bothering with these precautions because despite them all there is still an appalling climb in numbers for this infectious virus. I get that if we weren't doing these things – it would be 1446, or 2446, or 3446…. or worse but even so. I also know that these are numbers that other countries are seeing. So, I get it dear diary, on that matter I really do. I don't get why we are 18 months into this and still only at about 30% vaccination, or some other prophylactic but that's another matter.

What I am concerned about today, dear diary, is something far more important. Far, far more important.

I recall a few years ago an ex-Chief of Air Force once told me that he thought some coffees were a 'why bother?' and he was correct. He explained that a regular coffee is fine, and he included in this that the derivatives and alternatives of cappuccino, latte, piccolo etc… they are fine too. His righteous objection was to the watered-down nonsense that appeal to some people, the semi-skim, decaf, half water, half strength, lo-fat, sweetener, one scoop of caramel, type of orders that we see. Those are not coffee. Coffee is strong, black (within reason) and contains caffeine. It gives a buzz. He maintained that the 'why bother' changes the taste and more importantly, the effect considerably. His point is valid. Why would you bother, if you want a skim coffee milk shake – off you go, buy that.

However, my question today reaches further than even the importance of coffee. A beverage of which I've had two this morning already, so the keys are on fire as my fingers wage unrelenting war on the laptop! No, my concern today is far more important. It is the ridiculous 'why bother' of people offering an Australian Firefighters Calendar, wait for it, that is an animal only version.

Animals only? Why bother?

I am unable to suitably convey the infuriation at this complete brain check. Who thought a firefighter's calendar, animals only, edition was a great idea? What rocket scientist dreamt up this idea? I know COVID is affecting people adversely, but this is beyond the worst impacts. Beyond, dear diary…

I haven't had breakfast yet, but I think scrambled eggs are required to console me. How much vodka do you normally put into scrambled eggs, dear diary?

Sigh, 466. Until tomorrow…..

Lock-Down-Under - Day 51 - just taking a chill pill...

Hello my dear diary,

It's been a lovely day so far. A great night sleep, window tightly shut, with blackout blind down meant a deep slumber until 8.30. Oh man, how relaxed a person feels after a sleep like this. This was followed by coffee and a little TV in bed, then out for a walk.

I'm all about efficiency dear diary, so I combined my walk with my weekly shopping trip and the journey involved some very picturesque little streets in Inner West Sydney on route to Marrickville. Less than 20 minutes later I was out with all my goodies and heading for home.

I am now laying on the sun lounger on my balcony indulging in a cheeky little gin and tonic.

I mean, dear diary, who really cares about the NSW COVID cases being at 415 today?? Yep.... not me. I am deciding not to care. Yep, the decisions we make.

Ah well, until tomorrow.... but I do wish I had a bubble buddy to refill my drink. Where's Hugh, hot UK ex or any Australian Firefighter when you need one?

Gets up to wash that ornament to use as a gin bath

Lock-Down-Under - Day 52 – COVID Canine Contingencies Matter Too

Oh, ffs dear diary.

This morning's walk in the park seemed to be dog paradise. How are we ever going to get through this when there is a pack of five pooches all over each other on their morning ablutions! I mean think about it! How are we ever gonna get past this impact and spread of COVID when all these pooches are flaunting ALL the restrictions just willy-nilly. It was like a furry mosh-pit for heaven's sake in addition to all those owners enabling this pooch paradise get together.

Some of these animals got a bad attitude, Scooby! No wonder todays NSW COVID figures are at 478.

Yes, that's right dear diary. Four. Seven. Eight. Just when we think we've seen our worst day at 466, this tops it, and this isn't the end of it. I suspect we will be over 500 in the next week. Merry Bloody Christmas NSW! Strap yourself in as we may still be here then.

However, animals and COVID cases aside. I am loving my morning sojourn through the beautiful park located opposite me. I found myself singing on the way there this morning.

I can't recall if it was Blur or Oasis that sang 'ParkLife' but I found myself murdering it, quite comprehensively, as I skipped in a happy-go-lightly way that I hadn't undertaken since I was, well, Happy and Go-Lightly. But that was many, many, many years ago. I have to admit now that it was more a murder of the song than singing, especially as multiple 'doo' 'doo' and 'da' followed by a loud "PARKLIFE" can't ever, even with my imagination, be classified as doing justice to this piece of music.

I have to say dear diary, that whilst I spend about 20-30 minutes each day making light of lockdown and the severity of it, I am not immune or blind to other things going on in the world right now.

My heart goes out to the people of Afghanistan as the coalition withdraws and for the people. Their world changes again and again they prepare to live in a very restricted, fundamentalist way. After twenty years of something akin to freedom or at least freedom of choice, it's about to change. I think about the amazing people I met there and hope, above all hope that they are okay.

I am mindful about the number of deaths we are seeing, not just here, but worldwide.

I am mindful on the impact of people's mental health.

I am mindful on the impact of small businesses (and the bigger ones).

And I am cognisant that when we come out of this, eventually, the world may be a different place. But we can't see or predict this now. How could we ever have predicted this? Never mind the repercussions of it.

Whether else is occurring around the world; a world separating families, uprooting businesses, costing money, costing lives, it makes us more aware of our own personal space, more fearful of travel or more grateful for what we have. I don't know the outcomes; I just know I'll be different and I'm not Robinson Crusoe there. Just how different is yet to be seen.

Anyway, dear diary, until tomorrow. Until tomorrow, when I'll be a whole new woman with something changed. I'm sure of it.

Lock-Down-Under - Day 53 - where's it gone?

Sorry diary lovers.

Today was a busy day.

I need food.

And I need to get back to computer as I have more work to finish.

NSW COVID cases today, 453....ah, crap!

Lock-Down-Under - Day 54 – asked and now answered

I'm a little off topic today dear diary.

I spent time in Afghanistan. My time there was eight years ago and for a period of nine months. It was during the transition period handing the infrastructure back to the Afghanis and similarly to Iraq, it was an honour to assist helping with that transition. But only when people have the right to choose their destiny.

Having spent a few days being asked questions about how I feel about the events in Afghanistan with the previous leaders overtaking the country again, I thought I'd take the time to answer them.

How do I feel dear diary? Well, I feel how I imagine the majority of my military mates from all over the world feel right now. I feel sick, stunned, sad but somehow surprised and not surprised all at once.

When I served in Afghanistan, it was a large chunk of my Military service, and I was the Base Commander of Tarin Kowt. It was a base of 7,500 people ranging from USAF, US Army, 2000 contractors, 1000 Afghan National Security Forces (ANSF) including one of their Special Operations Brigades, 500 'terps' or interpreters and around 1000 Aussies. It was a surreal time and one I will remember forever.

I also had the privilege of meeting some extraordinary, wonderful people. In this category, I exclude the one I smuggled into my room for a few nights of fun. Despite the fact he had all the physical characteristics and appearance of hot UK ex, he wasn't all that wonderful, dear diary! No, when I speak about wonderful, I mean the Afghan men that we were working in partnership with to hand over the Base after the withdrawal of our troops from Uruzgan Province at the end of 2013.

I made a comment about these guys at the time. I said that, despite the fact I got my arse handed to me at chess within 20 minutes (and I have been playing chess a long time) they were some of the most spectacular people I had ever met. I mentioned that it warmed my heart to know there were people like this here *in Afg*. I mentioned that I had hope because if the country was in their hands, it would have a great future. Look at how wrong I was, dear diary.

But should we be shocked now? Why should we be indignant now and irate. We saw this coming, and our respective governments did very little that we can see. On my website, in the image carousel are some images of the Taliban occupying increasingly more regions of Afghanistan over the past few years. The source is the Australian Broadcasting Corporation and we, as a coalition, saw this coming and stood by. That is why I am sad. Two decades of work and a generation of people enjoying a freer society, catapulted back to a time they hoped to never revisit and wanted to forget. That is why I am sad.

Finally, I have been continually asked how I coped.

I coped the way I always cope. I coped the way I did in Iraq and Sudan. I coped the way I am doing now, through this lockdown alone.

I coped by doing what I could. When I couldn't, by writing a diary and blogs and, in the Afghanistan scenario, distracting myself by buying stuff online. Amazon was my drug of choice, followed by the amazing Turkish Tailor who had a shop on the base, catering to all of us there. So many people have commented on the various Ivanka Trump shoes and stunning, designed by Lee, wool coats I brought home with me, along with a gift of an Afghan wedding dress. In fact, despite this being a long time ago, I am still wearing the shoes and the coats and treat them like the precious jewels they are.

Oh, and by the way, NSW COVID cases today were 633 but today, who the hell cares?

Until tomorrow, dear diary, until tomorrow....

Lock-Down-Under - Day 55 – defining a COVID kilo

On average, a Panda feeds for approximately 12 hours per day. This is probably the same as an adult at home under quarantine, which may be why we call it a "Pandemic"

Ouch, dear diary, and I made such a great start.

Lots of walking, lots of self-discipline and lots of wellness time combined with the usual, lots of work. But somewhere the balance is going astray.

At the outset of this latest outbreak, when it was reported as being in the Eastern Suburbs, the rumour was the bulk or panic buying was focused on cocaine, Botox and gluten free bagels. Presumably then a COVID kilo was the amount of cocaine one consumed during lockdown, but for me the COVID kg seems to be the traditional old way – yep, dear diary, weight gain.

I shouldn't be surprised as, after a long time away from a regular glass of wine each evening, I've reconsidered that way of living and I'm back into it. In my defence dear diary, it's regulated and not guzzling, unless I am on a Zoom catch up, drinking meeting with Bel, Kyles or Manda. It's usually just the one glass unless it's the aforementioned event, in which case it has been known to resemble an "all bets are off" and the best part of half a bottle. Thankfully no more than that. Not back to the bad old days of overindulgence of booze. But that's another story for another day.

I've also noticed an increased amount of chocolate appearing in my shopping trolley and shifted swiftly into my fridge. Yeah, it's now noticed and about to be a lesson learned as it won't be being replaced. This isn't a rabbit hole I want to go down, Alice. However, I certainly won't be throwing it out, I mean I am Scottish after all and still have the first penny I ever earned. Every penny is a prisoner with me! This chocolate will be consumed, but like everything – apart from COVID – in moderation.

I'm also intent on actually taking a lunch break today, but that's only as I am meeting the wonderful Mel and we are buying our weeks supply (four tins) of Poor Toms pre-mix Negroni.

Speaking of a week's supply of something, I am sure the NSW COVID cases today were a weeks' worth, as if we are at 633 cases again today then we are in a world of hurt! Yep, world, get out the band-aids! NSW COVID cases were 681.

Sigh, until tomorrow, dear diary. Until tomorrow…

Lock-Down-Under - Day 56 – what girls yearn for....

Oh, dear diary,

This pissed me off a little.

Yep, I know you're now asking what the hell pissed me off. I know that you know my irritation is often just for effect and entertainment, but I also know that you know, this is a point that needs to be made. It really is dear diary.

As is the point that all this, knowing me, knowing you, sounds like the diary version of the ABBA song! I get that but stay with me.

Today I saw it. I was in the Playgirl Penthouse Room of Pleasure. Last used for pleasure? God only knows when. It wasn't a cheesy Brit TV show that was the tipping point here today, it was something else. It was actually when I saw a post on FaceTube that just tipped me over the edge.

There is a FaceTube page called Girls Love Travel. It's an exceptionally supportive page for, well, female travellers. It's great. It's safe. It's informative. Folks have found travelling companions, accommodation, tourist tips on the site, indeed all sorts of very helpful stuff.

Today I found frustration. It was, dear diary, complete frustration. Why? Why? I hear you all scream. Well funny you should ask. It's because I saw a post today about a lady heading to Machu Picchu in three weeks' time. THREE WEEKS TIME? I'll be lucky if I get outside my front door in the next three months, never mind get to my planned trips of Queensland, Darwin or Tasmania. *shakes head*

However, it's not all bad. Tonight, by the magic that is Zoom, I'll be heading to a K-6 disco. For those not in Australia, that's a Kindy or Kindergarten to Year 6 disco! The beautiful young students have been making outfits for weeks. The outfits are to be based on bright colours and sparkles with the inclusion of glow sticks wherever possible. I seriously can't wait.

And I'm going to dress up too, dear diary. I've actually decided to put on a bra, just in case I frighten the kids!

Some other great news, NSW COVID cases today were 644 – so 37 less than yesterday. But the bad thing now is VIC had 50 and ACT 12. This ain't going away anytime soon.

Tonight's commiseration is red wine and a nice rogan josh that I intend to make whilst dancing with the kids!

Until tomorrow, dear diary. Until tomorrow....

Lock-Down-Under - Day 57 – a record in mediocrity

Ah, dear diary,

Let's hit the high points first.

A great night sleep. Waking up late. Feeling rested. Intermittently doing chores whilst drinking lemon and ginger tea and reading. A little bit of watching the news. And a stunning set of numbers for NSW COVID today and not in a bloody good way, it's 825.

Eight hundred and twenty-five cases. Eight hundred and twenty-five. And lockdown is now until the end of September. Yes, dear diary, it's you and me for at least another six weeks. How good does it really get?

So based on all of this, I've cancelled my flights to the Gold Coast. I've cancelled the hotel in Darwin. The hotel on the Gold Coast was already cancelled but because I am the eternal optimist, I am leaving the November trip to Tasmania as active. A girl should have something to look forward too, for heaven's sake. So, it's Tasmania and Hugh Jackman as my bubble buddy. The latter yet to be confirmed as he hasn't answered any of my pleading email missives.

The other thing though is one can always rely on FaceTube to bring up memories that make you smile. Five years ago, today, I was sitting in First Class in my travelling gear, with carry-on only and heading to Central America for a month, followed by home to UK. The essential piece of information here is that it was only with carry-on. A skill I am refining is the ability to travel for long periods with a small (ish) backpack.

These memories made me smile this morning as I read some of the original posts. Including the one with the man rolling cigars. Cigars being an indulgence and better tasting when rolled on a virgin's thigh, so the legend goes. The guy I met on my trip, whose photos came back today as a memory, well he refused my offer of assistance! Some of these cigar rollers have got a bad attitude.

It's early afternoon and I think it's time for breakfast, as the grumble I just heard wasn't the dishwasher, it was my tummy. Yep, a nice gin and tonic and some scrambled eggs.

Until tomorrow, dear diary. Until tomorrow…

Lock-Down-Under - Day 58 – having a boy look

Oh, dear diary,

Mea culpa, mea maxima culpa.

I really did have a boy look for something over the last few weeks, or more accurately, multiple boy-looks.

What and why?

I decided that lockdown was going to be a time I would do some renovations around the apartment, and the living room feature wall that was a textured steel grey was on the list to be refreshed. I had redone the bedroom about a year ago and it brightened it tremendously and so it was the living room next. It was on the list, and I was a woman on a mission. If only I knew the colour of the rest of the room. I had a paint colour card and if I could find it, I'd be giggling. But I couldn't find it, dear diary. I simply couldn't find it and I'd looked a few times. So, it was now starting to become annoying and not a little inconvenient.

I am not good with things like this. When it comes to my home and possessions I am, quite simply, OCD. I like everything in its place. I don't put wet towels on my bed. I don't throw my clothes on the ottoman. I never leave cups and glasses at the side of the bed. And I don't lose things.

Having said that though, I nearly lost my mind a few years ago when I misplaced a beautiful Swarovski pen that a friend had given me as a birthday gift. I was beside myself and turned out all my 'pen storage' areas looking for it. It was my mother, whom I affectionately call The Oatmeal Savage, that was the voice of reason! Aren't all mothers? She calmed me down from my upset telling me it would turn up and she was right. When I changed handbags a few months later there it was, all beautiful and sparkly and rose coloured. It hasn't left my sight since. But this paint card was elusive, and I didn't want to wait six months, so once again I was into the drawer I knew I'd filed it in and turning everything upside-down.

Eureka!!!

There it was, safely stored along the side of the little white plastic square box where I store, among some small handy tools, the paint tin openers! Country beige, I was in possession of the colour I needed. In the nick of time, just as the NSW Govt decided that Bunnings was no longer essential as a shop, I slipped in at the last minute. Two litres of paint, a couple of drop sheets later and I was ready for a day of getting messy and sweaty with a roller. Which is certainly not as sexy as it sounds, dear diary.

With the fury and determination of a frustrated woman locked in her apartment for nearly two months, I painted all through the announcement of NSW COVID cases today. Could be 833 or maybe 844. Who knows?? It's just surreal numbers right now. Probably enhanced by yesterday's protest and a pile of critics pontificating how Western Sydney is being treated differently to the eastern suburbs. Yeah, maybe – but maybe if they behaved differently. Working in Western Sydney I witnessed firsthand the blatant violation of the rules in some of the areas being discussed. Cafes with no masks, including the guys serving food and crowds sitting outside like nothing was going on in the world.

Then, I pause to compare it to the frenzy of the Northern Beaches residents last Christmas. This frenzy and breaking of the Health Guidelines causing a requirement to deploy NSW police. Barricades were erected and a general blocking of the roads in and out of that area. The powers that be and their single-minded determination to reduce transmission despite the fact it was Christmas. I guess now we are getting what we deserve.

Anyway, its 6pm here and post a painting shower and nap, I've grabbed a glass of wine and two ibuprofens as my back is bloody killing me. Youth is wasted on the young.

Until tomorrow, dear diary. Until tomorrow...

Lock-Down-Under - Day 59 – the wee things that make me smile.

Oh, dear diary,

I could start this daily diary missive with a comment about hot UK ex here but there are lots and lots of other things that make me smile, dear diary. And things that more accurately resemble the description of 'wee'; cos 6'3" would never be described accurately as wee.

On Friday, as I wrote about, it was the Kindy – Year 6 disco and it was truly magnificent. On todays normal Monday morning meeting with my team, we spent a good ten minutes speaking about how delighted and excited the students were. I took some video footage and sent it to friends and family amusement, but it was short and needed to ensure that the kids weren't identifiable. The lengths we must go to for the protection of children. Of course, we should. We need to protect the innocent, but I would have loved to share more of the joy of these young humans at an online disco. It made my face hurt smiling and sharing their joy.

I do have to say though dear diary, I am not in love with the Baby Shark song as it can become quite annoying and really, really quickly. However, I was laughing so much at YMCA, mainly at the parents dancing, that I missed taking a photo of it. It was simply brilliant and a highlight of my week. The Senior Leadership Team were all 'at' the disco and I was the only one that didn't have my camera on. The no camera option was because I was cooking and an image of a red wine drinking, bad dancing, Scottish Woman wielding a large kitchen knife wouldn't have been good for the overall atmosphere!

I am also happy as it's getting warmer. Summer is coming and thumbing its nose at Winter. At 6.30 this morning I asked Google what the temperature was. She replied, "today the temperature in Alexandria is 19 degrees". Oh, goodie, 19 degrees. When I worked at Portland Naval Air Station, I'd be on Weymouth beach at that temperature! In a bikini. That's classified as UK tropical! With only five minutes until park meeting time, I stripped off the thermal, waterproof jacket and went for a lighter sweater. It's going to be a good day, dear diary. It's off to a great start.

Seriously though, how good is the start of the warmer weather? Spring is a week away (1 Sep) but it's great to feel the cold receding. I should have known it was going to be warm today as it was very mild overnight, and I found myself crawling from one side of the bed to another to find some cooler spots. My bed is 6 ft and 6 in wide (oh gosh, both hot UK ex and Hugh, not together obviously, would have space to spare - sigh) so it's quite the nightly exercise getting from one side to the other; even without obstacles. And here, in the absence of Hugh Jackman as my bubble buddy, I suppose a good rolling alone seeking cooler sheets will need to do!

Talking about being rolled, NSW COVID cases today were 818. Are we seeing a drop after the peak?

Well, I bloody doubt it as 1000s of protesters took to the streets of Sydney and Melbourne today to protest. Don't get me wrong dear diary, I am not condoning or condemning them. Neither do I condone the fact we are shut off from the rest of the world, or that we have effectively imposed Marshall Law on our communities. This is all in addition to the issue that we have police using weaponry on our own citizens, here in Australia. Unfortunately, whilst we have idiots running rampant and spreading this bloody virus, the Govt will continue to tighten these restrictions and most likely, the enforcement of them. What else can they do?

Would we have been better going hard early on vaccinations and herd immunity? Maybe. But we didn't and here we are. It will be interesting to see how things go when we do reach the 70 and 80 percent vaccination targets.

Ah well, I've now finished listening to the Glad Wrap, as the daily missive from the Premier Gladys Berejiklian has been nicknamed, and it's back to work.

Until tomorrow dear diary, until tomorrow…

Lock-Down-Under - Day 60 – tempting fate

Dear diary,

Holy snapping duck shit Batman, did I mention a potential spring or even summer the other day? Did I jinx that one dear diary?

When I looked out the window at lunch yesterday it was grey. Just miserable and grey. So, I turned to the oracle that is Google.

"Hey Google, what's the chance of rain today in Alexandria"

Google tells me dispassionately "there is an 80% chance of rain from 3pm!"

So that's it. It's been raining since. Persisting down, in fact. I went to bed last night with every intention of walking in the rain this morning. Why not? I have all the gear and my hair needed to be washed anyway, so what did I care? However, at 6am when I heard it pelting down on the roof, even a tractor ridden by Hugh Jackman couldn't have gotten me out of bed.

Yeah, I grabbed my computer, in fact I grabbed both computers, personal and work, and started work about 6.30. From bed. Why not? I think a few people were surprised at receiving emails quite so early, some were even more surprised at the lack of errors!

Now it's approaching 4pm and I think I am done for the day. There is a lamb roast, with veggies, on the agenda alongside a glass of red wine to accompany it. It will be a nice change for a glass of red as this week has been mainly a nice gin and tonic. One alcohol misadventure though was the not-so-easy to love strawberry gin, sour beer. I bought this experiment with my Negroni Spritz purchase last week. Hmm, yep, the jury's out on this one.

But speaking of all things sour, NSW COVID cases today are 753 with another 60 or so infectious in the community. You must hand it to the Victorians; they are keeping it at a cheeky 50ish – long may they contain this.

So, with the oven at 180 degrees, I'm launching in a couple of carrots and a slice of pumpkin, until tomorrow dear diary. Until tomorrow....

Lock-Down-Under - Day 61 – the law of large numbers…

Nope, dear diary,

I am not speaking of the NSW COVID cases today.

Maybe I should be talking about the COVID cases today though as they are an enormous 919 cases with over 700 being investigated because they don't know where the hell they've come from. No dear diary – that ain't it, but it bloody well should be! For the love of the wee man, no not hot UK ex, or Donny Ricardo for that matter, a massive 919 cases is just ridiculous. Furthermore, some news articles are forecasting over 2000 daily cases! Holy snapping duck shit once more, Batman.

Maybe the numbers are in line with the number of words I write in my diary each day! Maybe it's me. Maybe I'm the Jonah! Nah. The Oatmeal Savage always maintains I'm a lucky wee shite. And who really can argue with being referred to as a fortunate, whilst somewhat small piece of effluent!

No, the large numbers I am referring to come from many other places:

- The ten tickets from the four million for that apartment raffle in Coolangatta meant I had Buckleys chance of a win. This is a perfect example of how the law of large numbers works, or more accurately doesn't in my case of owning a new apartment.

- Checking every invoice at work has reaped rewards to the tune of $30,000 in overbilling and so reduced costs found, in today alone. Bring on tomorrow as I'm very, very ready to have another crack at it.

- When the accountant catches you out for additional consultancy income and you have to pay the blooming tax man, rather than receiving a refund, for the first time in 23 years

These are the good and bad large numbers I'm speaking about.

Tonight, small numbers, in fact a repeated one as I'll be having the third of four strawberry gin sour beers that I bought last Wednesday. Also, making an appearance for the second night running there will be a couple of cheeky carrots (as opposed to normal carrots) and a slice of pumpkin will also be on the horizon.

What more can a locked-up girl ask for? Until tomorrow dear diary. Until tomorrow….

Oh, and for those geeks out there that were really interested in the actual definition of the law of large numbers, if only to show that I'm using it out of context. In fairness, I know that.

In probability theory, the law of large numbers (LLN) is a theorem that describes the result of performing the same experiment a large number of times. According to the law, the average of the results obtained from a large number of trials should be close to the expected value and will tend to become closer to the expected value as more trials are performed.

Lock-Down-Under - Day 62 – a walk on the wild side…

Oh, dear diary,

I quite like the area I live in; you can get exercise and get high in the same timeframe. Not that I have ever indulged in drugs or any other illegal substance dear diary, oh no, not I.

That was pretty much assured because of my reaction to two things – smoke and needles.

As a young girl I fanatically hated cigarette smoke and would go so far to even give boyfriends an ultimatum; fags or me sweetheart, you choose but you can't have both. Principles, and acceptance that I was prepared to walk away from something I couldn't live with. This was compounded throughout my life by a passionate fear of needles and a lovely little habit of crumpling up on the floor/bed/chair/whatever else is handy, when faced with the thought of one going into my body.

Yep, no small pricks, without consequence for me!

Imagine my joy then a few years ago, when based with the army, I find myself one morning encountering a mutton fingered git who needed seven attempts to try and find a vein in my arms, and wrists, and then dear diary, was about to start on my ankle!

No bloody way, mate. Referral to Pathology in town please. Now.

All this has contributed to the smug knowledge from my parents that I would never touch drugs. Well, that and the promise by my father of breaking all my fingers! But walking round my 'hood you can smell it from nearly every third or fourth house. So, I've often wondered how this would affect when my morning walks continually, but not deliberately, ventures past these homes. Would I come home a little lightheaded. I think maybe that was my issue earlier today.

Taking delivery of a parcel this morning, I cut it open and initially saw what looked to be some gold, cheap, tacky, slinky material. Maybe the type you'd see articles from a sex shop wrapped up in. Well, so my friends tell me the paper is like.

It caused me to pause and ask myself, "What the hell did you drunk purchase now?" Are you stoned?

But no, it was the bootleg jeans I couldn't live without. I desired them as my skinny jeans don't work well with my pink cowboy boots. Also, I'm going to work tomorrow so the jeans and boots are gonna be pulled on early to make me feel happy! I mean, who doesn't turn to pink cowboy boots for happiness, dear diary?

But speaking of getting your leg pulled. Yeah, we keep hearing dates about lessening restrictions, but I bloody doubt it. NSW COVID cases today, 1029. Yep, we broke one thousand. From 150,000 tests. The majority (80%) are in western and south-western Sydney. Fan-bloody-tastic, I think not. The positive side of it though is the continuation of record numbers – 6.2 million of NSW are vaccinated and yesterday alone 156,000 jabs were delivered. Maybe by Christmas…maybe.

Anyway, dear diary, I'm going to unwrap these new jeans and hope they fit over my COVID enhanced arse! Until tomorrow my old friend, until tomorrow…..

Lock-Down-Under - Day 63 – a good sense of humour

Ah, Dear diary,

When you're divorced, dear diary, does any good story really start with "I remember one time, my husband......."?

No? Maybe? Well, I really do think that this one does. Yes sirree, for once I actually think it does.

Today however, a situation brought to mind a time when I recall the ex-OH regaling me with a story about the Squadron junior officers. These bright young guys, full of humour and mischief, had made up a song or poem, I can't remember which exactly, about two of the Squadron Executives. It was called The Ballad of Slicky Day and Des Madeira. This being a marvellously funny play on the nicknames of the two Executives; Oily Knight and Les Port. The piece of work waxed lyrical about these two men and some of the observations the guys had on them. It went into mannerisms and behaviours, it ridiculed small and large imperfections, it picked up these mannerisms exactly and I recall that at the time I thought it was hilarious. I wish I could remember the words but even just the title of Slicky Day and Des Madeira makes me smile in a Pavlovan type way.

This remembering of an old piece of mischief brings up another good point though. How good is a sense of humour?

I was exceptionally lucky to be 'raised' in the Royal Navy or more accurately the Women's Royal Naval Service, and apart from the fact that it taught me to drink like a Scottish fish and believe that Tourettes was a gift. It also exposed me (pun intended in many ways!) to the humour of 'Jack'. This humour is something that has been pretty much unsurpassed for the remainder of my career. Don't get me wrong, dear diary, I have met some exceptionally funny people since but never quite in the same quality or quantity that is the mixy-blob[1] of the Senior Service.

Having said that, it was three very funny, "special" guys that kept me sane through my time in Afghanistan; one US Navy and two Army chaps. Their friendship and humour was a bright light every day, and I am continually grateful that we are all still in touch. I am still subjected to the delights of their wit and sarcasm regularly. In fact one has just sent me a beer countdown clock https://www.timeanddate.com/countdown/party this is a little better than yesterday's gift which was a link to the naked Twister game rules!

I have found that as I have gotten older, and wiser, I still find that humour is an exceptional quality in a person. Previously I would look for intelligence, ability and potential in any next ex-husband candidates. But again, as I get older, I've decided that those are as

---

[1] Mixi-blob is a navy term when pieces of different colour are on the same square during a game called Ukkers.

rare as rocking horse poo. Moving the goal posts, I thought that a man with his own hair and teeth would be an acceptable alternative. Slim pickings too dear diary. Then when you throw a sense of humour requirement into the mix it becomes impossible. So, I'm gonna have to settle for Hugh Jackman after all. He just needs to get on board with my plan.

The community of NSW also needs to get on board with my plan for maintaining a sense of humour and a positive attitude as it's not going well at the minute. NSW COVID cases today are 882 from 118,000 tests. Vaccinations over the same period totalled 144,000 bringing the state up to 6.4m. Now this is all well and good but poor VIC are on 79 cases today. And QLD? Those lucky north neighbours are boasting a big fat zero with all their pubs and restaurants opening up from 4pm today; with dancing allowed. Have you seen me dancin' dear diary, I mean really dancin'? No, not for a while.

Anyway, another week in captivity has passed and I'm looking forward to a weekend of click and collect groceries and artificial green wall panels from Bunnings with some solar lights to thread through it. May as well have some aesthetically pleasing semi green areas to enjoy. There is no stopping my wildness this weekend.

Oh, and what was the situation that prompted all these thoughts and musings today? Yeah, weather and synthetic material are drying out my skin to the extent normal moisturiser isn't coping. So, I grabbed the re-gen skin oil and give the old pins a little treat with a slicky day and oily (k)night result.

Until tomorrow, and a quick drive through of Poor Toms gin pad on the way home to pick up some carry out Negroni cocktails! Scream! Until tomorrow....

Lock-Down-Under - Day 64 – I'd like to phone a friend, Eddy

Oh, dear diary,

If the question is "Who wants to be a millionaire?" then lock me right in.

But I guess for that to happen I have to buy lottery tickets, gotta to be in it to win it; and I don't. Sometimes I think about it and if I am in the vicinity of a newsagents when it's a big draw, I'll chuck over $12 but that is very infrequently. So, the closest I'll get to "millionaire" is phoning a friend. The reverse being them calling me, and that's what this week has been all about.

At the COVID outset I think the stress and uncertainty seemed to rub off badly on folks and I observed a fair bit of rudeness dear diary. I really did. And it was compounded by people hiding their shame behind masks. This time, whilst I see people getting frustrated, flat and a little sad, I see the same people banding together and helping each other in a sense of community. And whilst social media has its pitfalls, it is also a great means of community communication when being used for good; this seems to be the case around my area.

This time has also been a great opportunity to catch up with friends. So I, like many others, spend an inordinate amount of time on calls and Zoom catching up with as many of my friends as I can. It's bliss. I think I promised about 10 people I'd call them back this weekend and I'll try and fit some of them in. However, I'm trying to keep the phone clear for Hugh Jackman to call. And I hope it's today as Saturday is clean sheet day!

But these calls are obviously between the regular communication each morning and night from The Oatmeal Savage! God bless the oldies in UK. If we don't speak at least each night, she thinks I don't love her anymore or will ask if my phone is broken. At what age does the daughter guilt end?

I have also been humbled by the calls from other folks checking up on me. One this week was especially nice.

In March this year (2021), I went to a health retreat for a long weekend of vegetarian food, no alcohol, no caffeine, morning yoga and intense meditation with even more intense hypnosis. It seems like I do like to find other ways to torture myself since I am no longer in Defence and being emotionally tortured by those in that organisation, but it did start my enduring love of herbal teas. One of the other retreat inmates was a lady whose son had tragically killed himself. During one of the meditation sessions, we were asked to explain why we were there and what we wanted out of it. This lovely lady and her husband volunteered that since their son's death, they were abusing alcohol and were withering away from the sadness. It was heartbreaking.

As a group, we got to know each other well over that few days. In one of the discussions, I was asked about my life, my history and thoughts. I ventured my view of post deployment issues that were currently in the news and being a survivor which often entailed overcoming survivors' guilt.

It's like this.

I believe you have a moral responsibility to live your best life in memory of those who didn't return home. If you don't you may as well have died with them. I spoke sensitively knowing her dilemma and emotional challenges, but that I believed we owe it to those no longer with us. I think we do.

This lovely lady obviously found this to be a helpful and memorable statement because she phoned me this week to check on how I was, living alone in lockdown. She further reminded me of my words and told me that she and her husband had stopped daily drinking and were going to the gym (in the normal world) and plenty of walks in-between. She told me they were both doing well. I was in tears listening to her heartening story.

Look I think that was why I was in tears.

It also could have been that I spent all that hard earned Scottish money to pay for a health retreat to lose weight with the assistance of hypnosis and am still resorting to wearing stretchy arse pants! I'd have been more effective paying someone to break my jaw!

Anyway, speaking of things not working. NSW COVID cases today were a record of 1035. Over 156,122 people were vaccinated and 129,000 people were tested. Lock down to the end of September, my arse! We're in for the long haul as we've lost control of this. It's all over the place like a mad woman's shit.

I need a drink, and maybe some chocolate, can't think why I am not losing weight, sigh. Until tomorrow dear diary. Until tomorrow....

Lock-Down-Under - Day 65 – being like nana…

Oh, dear diary,

It has happened. It's finally happened. And a little earlier than I thought.

I suspected it would be a couple of decades before this occurred but no dear diary, there I was last night doing a bloody startling impersonation of my grandma! But there was no alternative, I was trapped, I was disgusted, and I couldn't do anything else but resort to behaving like an octogenarian.

What am I talking about? I know you're wondering dear diary, what was driving me so insane last night?

Well…… well it's about my feet. I have great feet. I have always had great feet. As a child the chiropodist told my mum I had great feet. I have feet protected persistently by wearing of slippers. Not so much right now, I'll give you the tip!

I thought back with longing at the dodgy little salon in Mascot, where you fight to get a parking space in the car park opposite. But when you find that elusive space, you feel so damn smug. It's also adjacent to a great liquor store, cake shop and the best Vietnamese Chilli Chicken Roll shop in the world outside Vietnam. Choices, choices and more decadent pleasure choices.

I digress as usual. Last night, I thought back to the lovely little nail salon with its lovely young women, where for the princely sum of $55 you get a magnificent mani/pedi. The mani is also with shellac that doesn't peel or chip; it lasts four weeks at a stretch. And then I though even more fondly of the 30 minutes or so that you get on one of those vibrating jiggly chairs. You know the ones; they fill you with warmth and give you far more pleasure than any ex! I've been a single girl for a long time, oh how I miss those chairs and maybe a bit of Hot UK ex too!

When I was in Iraq in 2003, my first time off after seven weeks was a girls afternoon get together. What we did was give ourselves a pedicure. Not as sexy as it sounds, it was just much needed female company and a little DIY attempt at pampering. That was part of the excitement and support I had over there throughout the deployment.

On this specific afternoon, there was five senior female officers, closeted away in a tent, combining our limited foot products and taking it in turns to soak tired feet in basins filled with hot water and washing powder. We knew how to live back then. We knew how to party and by God we were going to do it. A basin filled with washing powder and smelly boot feet.

This whole soaking feet in a basin was also something I had seen grandma do lots of times; so last night I knew it was time. I looked down with despair at my day 65 lockdown feet, then added the seven days prior since my visit to the salon, calculating that it's been two and a half months since they were properly attended to. The claw-like hooves that were looking back up at me from the freshly vacuumed carpet needed immediate attention.

The house had been the recipient of a complete scrub yesterday and now it was my turn. From the feet up!

In a matter of a few minutes later there I was, immersed up to the ankles in warm water and Fairy Liquid. My basin was balanced on a carefully folded towel, placed like the OCD nutter I am, to avoid any drips and spillage. I had looked out the 'tools' beforehand and I was ready to mutilate. I was a woman on a mission. And it felt bliss.

It somehow helps you sleep when your little tootsies are all nicely pampered and wrapped in some amazingly soft moisturizing sleep socks! Ah, now we're talking. The absolute bliss of it.

And that mellow, blissful mood remained right up until the NSW COVID cases were announced today. 1218. 1218.

My writing is about making fun of this ridiculous time in our lives, but I can't do it today. 80% plus of the cases are in Western Sydney and it's out of control. I understand the lockdown is no longer about trying to get to zero cases, but it's about minimising hospital cases now. We will never get to zero and we are all going to have to come to terms with this.

Our lives have changed, and it will not change back in the interim. Maybe it will never change back. I know it's changing me and my priorities. The freedoms we once enjoyed are now far on the distant horizon. My immediate priority, after health, is that I want to go home to Scotland and hug my parents. And also, to see all the Scottish men who surely look like the one on the calendar I received today!

Now though, it's time to treat me a little more. I'm gonna watch a bit of TV and I feel a nice glass of wine will go with it nicely. I think grandma would approve.

Until tomorrow, dear diary. Until tomorrow…..

Lock-Down-Under - Day 66 – just a quickie

Oh, dear diary,

That isn't anywhere near as sexy as it sounds.

Those were the days and now it's well and truly into the night!

Today is a busy day at 'school' with meetings from breakfast to a Board meeting that starts at 4pm and will still be going until 8pm. My main concern here is food and how I get it! In the spirit of being a good Defence Planner, or more accurately a great Dinner Planner, I've got tubs of soup ready that I can heat and surreptitiously eat via a mug!

I am taking a very quick break to listen to today's statistics and am watching it on-line. I swear to God, it looks like the Glad-Wrap crew are doing the walk of shame to the podium! It must be a bad set of numbers. Ah yes, and there they are.

NSW COVID cases today are another record of 1290 cases of community transmission with over 80% in Western Sydney. The better statistics are that in NSW there are 6.8m people with first jabs, which is 66% of population.

Back to the keyboard for me dear diary, until tomorrow….

Lock-Down-Under - Day 67 – oh, to just be a Strumpet

Oh, dear diary,

I am shaking my head today.

It should have been easy. It should have been very easy. But it wasn't and it isn't. I am changing my name. And it's gonna be Strumpet. I've decided. Just, well just cos….

I love technology and automation, dear diary, I really do. I love internet shopping. I love internet banking. I love the ability to look at tax records, health records, what I've been paid; I love it all; everything. I am an 'everything at the touch of a button, everything at your fingertips' type of girl. I really am. I absolutely am.

Today? Not so much. Today, I'm a 'launch the bloody computer out of the nearest window type girl' and by God, I'll do it soon.

This weekend, being a little behind on my linking of things, I tried to link MyGov to Medicare to get proof of vaccinations. I want those additional freedoms promised by the Fork Tongue Officials each day. It's surely a simple process, after all my tax is linked, Department of Veterans Affairs is linked as is Centrelink; Medicare will be a breeze. Or so I thought.

When moving to Australia years ago I was given a choice to make. Married name or maiden name. I chose de Winton and have continually struggled with the spelling since. To clarify, I have no issues with the spelling personally, but 70% of everyone else seems to just get lost in the complexity of the 'two words, small d' concept. I get everything from DeWinton, De Winton, Dewinton, De Wanton which is my personal favourite, de Winter which I also don't mind if it premised by Lady and accompanied by Four Musketeers.

So, the Australian Government call me DEWINTON, whilst Medicare likes to correctly call me DE WINTON. What's the difference? A space. And therein lies the problem; about 2mm of gap. Because the names are technically different, I am unable to link the accounts.

Name change? Searching through the FAQs, I find it's a common issue. The remedy? Call Services Australia. Yeah, not as easy as it sounds. Having been around the automation voice services three times and been kicked off three times on the "refer to MyGov" gateway message, I'll try online again. I mean I love technology, I'm an embracer of it. Yes, I am, I manage through gritted teeth.

Alternatives.

Name change via the Tax Office or Centrelink. It turns out Centrelink spells the name De Winton, and the Tax office needs an Australian Birth Certificate, Australian Marriage Certificate, or an Australian Legal name change document.

Name changed via Medicare. I venture into the darkness that is Medicare. Then miraculously, on my fourth call to Medicare, having been laughed at for wanting to mis-spell my name once and put through to the Immunization Cell the previous two, I finally found a lovely lady who said, "wait here, I'll see if I am allowed to remove the space in your name".

It's done. Finally done. A tidy little 68 minutes after I started this, I am finally done. If it had taken more than 90 minutes, I was changing my name to Ivanabea Strumpet; something nobody would forget! However, I have managed to write my daily diary, a variety of emails and complete three budget levy spreadsheets to send to the relevant Heads of Department: all whilst waiting patiently on calls. The other positive thing is that a glass of red wine at 8.30 before breakfast is totally acceptable in this sort of crisis, isn't it?

Now let's look at something else that is a shemozzle today. COVID NSW Cases today were 1164, with 67% of the NSW population injected with their first jab, and more importantly a brothel in Western Sydney has been closed down due to breaching Health Orders! LOL, a brothel. A brothel. I have no words. It took this long?

But all's well that ends well today, dear diary. Because at the end of the day, after all that, they have the correct spelling of my name on the vaccine certificate, and I have a pathway to freedom.

Until tomorrow dear diary, from your lovable little Strumpet. Until tomorrow...

Lock-Down-Under - Day 68 – tempus fugit

Oh, dear diary,

I keep being asked where I find the time.

Well, it's quite simple, dear diary; I have a lot of clocks. There are clocks everywhere in my apartment and the funkier the clock the more desirable to me. So, ergo, I have plenty of time.

Unfortunately, that time aplenty feeling became a little more restricted this weekend when the battery died on my watch. I love my watch. I love my watch so much, it's a cherished possession. It was purchased in 1993 and it's been on my wrist ever since. Ironically it was originally purchased for me by my ex-husband as I couldn't afford it at the time; and I then paid him back in monthly instalments until the debt was settled! Nope, I am not kidding.

However, back to the current issue of my dead battery; it's not really a problem as I have another watch. I bought it in 2013 as a little present to myself when serving in Afghanistan. I felt it was needed to accompany the ten pairs of shoes I accidently purchased in some of my nightly internet shopping extravaganzas on Amazon. I'm now thinking, I'll just go pull out the other watch. Yeah, if wishing made it so…. I now recall I had both watches serviced with replacement batteries at the same time a little over two years ago. Dagnamit. Now, no watch. No watch shops open. No sign of watch shops opening. And it's a hole in my life; I am running out of time; I think to myself a little hysterically. For those who, like me, wear watches permanently, have you ever tried a few days without one. It's a little inconvenient. It's a lot inconvenient. A First World problem, without a doubt, but bloody inconvenient, nonetheless.

The other part of time in the queries I received is where do I find the time to write these daily 'dits'. Yeah, that's an easy one. I generally have some admin to do in the evening, so I start drafting a few notes during the day on the events I see and do; then when Gladys announces her daily scores on the doors, this is ready to go.

If I haven't done it the night prior, then I'll stay behind after work and quickly draft it then, usually with a glass of wine. Today, it's 6.30am and I'm having a coffee in bed before a walk. I think it's important to do this as I will look back on this in years to come and recall the days locked in with humour. It's just not funny – yet. So here is yet another day, in all its sad heartbreaking splendour.

So, speaking of hitting the scores on the doors…. NSW COVID cases today were 1116. No more to add really!

And now it's time for me to get out the PJs, throw on some scruffy walking gear and go get some fresh air.

I am also a little giddy today as we are having a 'ridiculous hat' Zoom meeting this morning as part of our regular 8.30 Wednesday morning catch up at work. Until now I've asked the team to display background photos of their travels and they tell us about the photo during the meeting. It's like world travel voyeurism and a wonderful distraction for people who have been in lockdown for nearly ten weeks with a bleak four to six weeks to go. Some lovely memories being relived.

Anyway, enough from me today, time is finally up so until tomorrow, dear diary, until tomorrow....

Lock-Down-Under - Day 69 – a confused mind

Oh, dear diary,

I recall those days of trying, somewhat unsuccessfully, to structure an academic assignment.

Australian Command and Staff College in 2007, the first time I had been required to do some academic type assignments of this standard in, well, ever. It was indeed a tough year at times. I ran away at 17 to join the Royal Navy. I had done exams, to be sure. I had done sufficient exams to get me into my choice of category, but nothing like this. And if I am being honest, I'd avoided this type of no-operational, takes some deeper thinking, type of essay writing.

I can't be alone in that dear diary, I'm sure I'm not Robinson Crusoe there. I get that it had been decades since I had needed to do anything even remotely like this, so it was tough. But in the spirit of 'shy bairns get nothing' I asked for help.

It didn't take long for the academic to tell me that I had a little confused mind. Something any psychologist would back up wholeheartedly, I'm sure. But in the academic's opinion, my mind goes from A-Z too quickly and forgets the steps in between, more specifically, it forgets to explain the steps in between. Things work out in my head, and I know exactly how I got there but specifying this including the analysis of the journey, well that was a little more problematic. I know what I'm talking about – so isn't that enough, dear diary?

So, you can imagine how my confused frenzied, hyped up, little mind reacts to a variety of things. Today for some strange and inexplicable reason, it's the number 69. And I don't know what brought it to mind today. I certainly haven't been hiding Hugh under the sheets. Nope. Presented with that saucy figure, my confused, but self-confessed, quick mind goes a little wild. It conjures up all sort of nonsense. When younger, I couldn't think about it without tittering. I'm guessing I am not alone there and some of you may wonder what this is pertaining to. Sure, you are. Of course you are.

This tittering, however, degraded to a truly disgraceful snort laugh when attending Tranny Bingo for the first time. Being a connoisseur of bingo, I enjoy a good bingo calling. The snort occurred when the amazing Tranny Bingo host, Tora Hymen, called the number. "Two can dine, sixty-nine!" I nearly pee'd myself with spontaneous laughter. She's a risqué old tart, that Tora. Even more salacious at the annual Tranny two-up experience, which is a regular feature at The Bank Hotel in Newtown on ANZAC Day. This is an adventure not to be missed for the Sydney dwellers. Watching a heaving, delightfully happy crowd part with money on both alcohol and two up; all egged on by a 6ft 2 inch Tranny in 6" heels. How I adore her! In fact, on my website labelled for today, there's pictures of me adoring her! And her adoring my dad!

And that, dear readers, is a perfect example of the rabbit hole of A-Z my mind goes down.

What's even more confusing though is our lockdown and the captivity we find ourselves in. Unfortunately, the NSW COVID cases today are a cheeky 1288 cases from 121,000 tests and we are now over 7m jabs. There are still promises of opening international travel at 70% double dose, which is forecast for October. Is it just me that thinks, you speak with forked tongue?

On the brighter side, only one more day until the weekend and on day 70, I'll be doing my weekly negroni trip to Poor Toms Distillery.

So, until tomorrow, dear diary, until tomorrow…

Lock-Down-Under - Day 70 – a bright spark

Well, dear diary,

It is now ten weeks and no sign of immediate relief.

The brighter side is that each day is filled with another little shard of joy and often something else to ridicule or just poke fun at. Today was funky scarf day on our morning video conference, and I pulled out an old feather boa. It probably wasn't the best choice for a variety of reasons.

Some things you need to know if you own a feather boa and if it's the same as in this case, it's more than a few months old.

-   They shed more than a Pyrenean Mountain Dog. One teeny, tiny, slight bit of air when I opened the back door and there were bloody green feathers everywhere. It was like someone had murdered a Fraggle. In the end it looked like it had snowed green, all over my study and even worse than the snow were the little bits of the fibres that were spread all over my black t-shirt. I resembled a green and black micro dot Dalmatian.

-   They itch. Those feathers are tickly little creatures. Both over your skin and up your nose. Yep, they got everywhere. You breath and suddenly you're sneezing, ticklish green snot.

-   The are jaggy. Aside from the itching, the hard stems of the feathers stab you. Feather boas are vicious!

But aside from my discomfort and alien like nasal issue, it was hilarious to see most of this morning's participants in a variety of scarves, and like the background holiday pictures previously, each scarf had a story behind it. It is lovely to hear these interesting snippets about my team.

As the Director of Business Operations, I also look after Enrolment, Administration, IT, Facilities Management, Cleaning, Marketing and Communications and Finance, so there are always a wide variety of interesting stories aside from holidays, hats and scarves. The one that had us aghast today was an email from a parent with a request.

Due to home schooling, her kids were eating more, they were using more water and using more electricity. Would the school be willing to compensate them for this difference? She even suggested an amount. Seemingly $250 per week would do it. So effectively we are paying her to educate her children. I get to make these return calls, sometimes, just sometimes I shake my head. It was a nice try though, and I do get her point. My home electricity, water, grocery, and to a certain extent alcohol bills are nearly out of control.

The opposite of this though is from a business perspective, all these bills were significantly lower. Some businesses, not aviation, that can maintain productivity and revenue with a working from home model, must be rubbing their hands at their significant savings. Just an observation!

Speaking of other things that make you shake your head NSW COVID cases today 1431. Yep, it's a spectacularly crappy effort. With worse figures predicted in the next two weeks. The addition to this though is the number of lives being lost to this virus. Figures also being reported daily. Not good.

I am just so pleased my fambam are safe even although they are so far away.

But the brightest light today is a trip to Poor Toms for a Negroni Spritz pick up. See you at 5.30 Mel!

So, from me dear diary, lets chat again tomorrow. Until then....

Lock-Down-Under - Day 71 - running with scissors

Oh, dear diary,

This old lockdown thingy gives you a bit of time to think, so it does.

It gives time to recognise what you do. It gives you time to realise how you behave.

Fixing myself a nice refreshing drink a few days ago and not having any little cocktail umbrellas and cherries to decorate it, I popped in a stainless-steel straw. I was chatting online to a friend at the time and mentioned how the little things can be enjoyable, things like these inexpensive straws.

But her view differed a little.

She had read a report of some unfortunate lady who had tripped and been fatally wounded due to these straws. Don't worry I advised my friend; I was warned about running with sharp objects as a child! I'm very careful.

It turns out that I am really not. Having this image and warning at the forefront of my mind, it would appear that when I consciously thought about my actions, I am the world's worst culprit. I am the biggest multitasker! If this means eating or drinking or cutting something whilst walking. I bloody do it. I'm as guilty as a puppy sitting next to a pile of poo!

Now I have visions of injuring myself and because I live alone, it conjures up that scene from Bridget Jones. It's the one scene at the beginning where Bridget is tipsy and reflecting with wine and music, and her thoughts are of being found dead, eaten by Alsatians, listening to Chakka Khan.

However, I don't think that that would happen to me as The Oatmeal Savage calls every night. One missed call and she'd be right over here, most likely on her broomstick, dad as the pillion passenger. Just kidding Patsy!

Anyway, speaking about piles of poo. NSW COVID cases today are 1533. Buckle up folks, it's a rough ride.

To make it gloomier, it's a rainy afternoon in Sydney but, but, but this week Ch7 screened The Greatest Showman. It's almost as if the Gods wanted to bring Hugh Jackman into my living room!

Scream...if only he were naked too.

Gotta go, Hugh is waiting. Until tomorrow, dear diary. Until tomorrow......

Lock-Down-Under - Day 72 - the path to hell....

Oh, dear diary,

It was all great and the intent was there on Saturday night, ah ha, it was a plan!

Yep, I was going to get up early and check the Aldi stores around me for the cordless screwdriver I missed out on in Marrickville yesterday. But two cups of coffee and four episodes of the latest binge watch later, I was having the morning in bed. And it was bliss, completely bliss.

Who on earth needs another cordless screwdriver anyway?

Not this sleepy bed hogging chick!

It's a beautiful day, so post my leisurely morning it's been home pottering and chores. I love my apartment, especially when it's lovely clean and tidy. I foresee a stunning afternoon reading on the balcony in the spring sunshine!

Now talking about the path to hell being paved with good intentions, this current lockdown futility. I'm sure there was some good intent. If only everyone's intent was pure! Nah, and the result? NSW COVID cases today were 1485. And again, we're warned that the worst is to come.

One word for this today. F*ck.

Thank goodness there's a Negroni left from my weekly stash! Until tomorrow dear diary. Until tomorrow...

Lock-Down-Under - Day 73 – yeah, and there's the line....

Oh, dear diary,

These con artists have no tact or decorum.

Today, I received a few texts from numbers I don't recognise. The texts are about deliveries, and I can't remember what I've ordered, when I ordered or actually if I ordered. If I did, it's not that much.

One little gadget from Amazon and two new face masks do not six texts, with four different pathways to click-on, make! Oh no. Yeah, press here for delivery cos you found a parcel from August, my lily-white arse. This COVID internet shopping frenzy is allowing all sorts of new Nigerian princes to emerge.

The latest in the line of the unsubtle happened last night in the form of this e-mail. This was the one that tickled me. It would have done more if I'd been undertaking the actions that I am being accused off.

> You may be asking yourself, "But my PC has an active antivirus, how is this even possible? Why didn't I receive any notification?" Well, the answer is simple: my malware uses drivers, where I update the signatures every four hours, making it undetectable, and hence keeping your antivirus silent.
>
> I have a video of you wanking on the left screen, and on the right screen - the video you were watching while masturbating. Wondering how bad could this get? With just a single click of my mouse, this video can be sent to all your social networks, and e-mail contacts.
> I can also share access to all your e-mail correspondence and messengers that you use.
>
> All you have to do to prevent this from happening is - transfer bitcoins worth $1450 (USD) to my Bitcoin address (if you have no idea how to do this, you can open your browser and simply search: "Buy Bitcoin").
>
> My bitcoin address (BTC Wallet) is:
> 1FbN9mgTzppSUGRgBs1o7N8FpPQVfoRrKd
>
> After receiving a confirmation of your payment, I will delete the video right away, and that's it, you will never hear from me again. You have 2 days (48 hours) to complete this transaction. Once you open this e-mail, I will receive a notification, and my timer will start ticking.

So having told you all, you are now in danger of receiving said video footage of me as per the threat. My team at work were delighted to hear me telling them about this email. They were even more amused, dear diary, when I explained that I never watch porn on my work computer. Or any computer, actually. I'm not sure if that makes me pure, naïve, or sad, but it does mean I can't be fooled by bad email attempts at extracting cash.

Taking about bad jokes and even worse confidence tricks. NSW COVID cases today were 5690. Not really it was 1281 but I suspect that's because it was Father's Day yesterday and there were lower testing rates. But maybe I'm just a cynical old masturbating cow!

It's late tonight and I am tired but wanted to finish writing this daily missive, as I hadn't done it last night. Compounded by the fact that I was in at work today. An hour journey, each way, certainly takes a bit out of your day when you're no longer used to it, doesn't it?

So, until tomorrow dear diary cos I'm off to watch some Hugh porn, X-Men. Until tomorrow....

Lock-Down-Under - Day 74 – is this really, right? For candles….

Well, dear diary,

I wonder if any of my friends received emailed deep fake videos of my supposedly saucy antics yesterday?

If so, I'd be interested in seeing them.

It would be good to know what happens in my bedroom (or sofa) and with my computer – when I'm not there. I wonder if the interloper doing all these naughty things has managed to link the picture sharing on either the living room or bedroom TVs. Technology that's defeating me, I'll give you the tip, dear diary. The luxury of watching Netflix and not on a four-inch phone screen sounds like bliss!

What didn't sound like bliss to some was the image I saw on FaceTube last night. In all fairness, I laughed more at the comments. Inner West Sydney is a great set of suburbs. We pride ourselves on being trendy, a little grungy, edgy, funky but not up ourselves. So, I have no idea what this FaceTube seller was thinking when she posted on the Inner West Buy Sell and Give Away PIF, trying to sell her Chanel No. 5 tiny, little, birthday cake candles for $50. "Pick up Double Bay, or AusPost at the buyers' expense" No wonder the comments were extreme. One being "white people must be stopped!". I laughed until my tummy hurt. Or maybe that was the excessively stuffed chicken salad wrap I had for dinner. Hmmmm.

Talking of outrageous figures, NSW COVID cases today were a surprising 1220. I'm not getting excited yet though. We still haven't seen the effect of the riot a few weeks ago.

However, on that note, I was a tad surprised at the comments made by the Dutch President. He went on the record in response to a protest by anti-vaxxers, saying that the rest of the country was injected and if these guys infected themselves, so be it. Maybe about time somebody said it!

Anyway, dear diary, our little tete-a-tete was a bit later today and for me it's time for a repeat offense of that chicken salad monstrosity from last night!

Until tomorrow, dear diary. Until tomorrow….

Lock-Down-Under - Day 75 – was it really in poor taste, or just very funny?

Oh, dear diary,

I really should pause for a few seconds longer before I speak.

In all fairness, it's always been an issue. Inside voice out loud and normally where angels fear to tread. I get that. It's something I have been working on extensively and I really thought I had it under control. Yeah, nah. Not today seemingly.

Today I was in a meeting dear diary. An important meeting. One of the women mentioned that for her COVID vaccination the nurse took one look at her larger-ish arm and stated that she only had a small needle. I know, I know. You can see it can't you dear diary, it was a train wreck that would have been visible from outer space.

Before I could shut the hell up, I piped up with "I used to be married to somebody like that! Apparently one of the symptoms of COVID is having no taste. Looking back on my exes, I think I've been infected for years"

And look I may have gotten away with my wee risqué remark, if one of the men hadn't physically snorted and spat coffee all over his computer. It wasn't a pleasant sight I'll tell you dear diary, yukky yukky. It also delayed the meeting by a few minutes until he could clean up his disgraceful spillage. Realistically though, it actually wasn't such a bad thing as I was getting to the 'poke my eyes out and rip my ears off' stage anyway!

Talking of train wrecks, 1480 COVID cases in NSW today. Geez, pleez…. alcohol time!

Until tomorrow, dear diary. Until tomorrow…

Lock-Down-Under - Day 76 – that would hit the spot…

Oh, dear diary,

It's as if these creeps that keep texting and offering things are listening into my conversations.

I know there has been a plethora of fake parcel tracking texts and I give those a good stiff ignoring, but a reduction on wine?? Oh, now you're talking. Who doesn't love a good alcohol deal?

And speaking of alcohol, dear diary. I am not a promotional tool for Poor Tom's Negroni Spritzers, but when the fourth person called to say they'd ordered some, I thought about asking for commission. But in reality, it's a good deed to the community of Australia in their time of need.

I have needs too! I mean, dear diary, in my weekly food shopping on Monday night, I found some Gin to go with the salad I was contemplating. I think it'll go with the yoghurt, strawberries, granola, steak and spaghetti bolognaise too! Victory is mine. Victory is mine.

Not so victorious is the 1405 NSW COVID cases today but there are some green shoots appearing. Specifically, that's 18 Oct, still six weeks away but it's restricted opening for double dosed people. Yippee that's me! However, let me tell you how the vaccinations are actually going. 294,651 doses were administered on 7 September 2021 (yesterday at the time of writing), which was the latest reporting period. 13,313,703 people have had their first dose. This is 51.98% of the total population or 64.57% of 16+. There are 8,186,949 fully vaccinated. This equates to 31.87% of all Australians, or 39.7% of age 16+. News today is that another 500,000 doses of the Pfizer vaccine have left the UK bound for Australia. Cheers Britannia!

For me tonight it's a swift drive home as I've been in the office today. It will definitely be via a car wash as Patsy is vile. That's the car, not The Oatmeal Savage.

So, until tomorrow, dear diary. Until tomorrow…..

Yeah, on reflection, day 76 in lockdown. This has got knobs on!

Lock-Down-Under - Day 77 – Friday exhaustion!

Oh, dear diary,

What a day. What a bloody day.

In fact, dear diary, what a week. Having been in a school for a few days this week and sometimes forgetting to stop work at a normal time, I am glad it's Friday. I'm now into my third gin, which is unusual as two is the limit these days, and I am ready for dinner and bed. However, it's been a hoot.

Back to today. We had two staff in the building designed for over twenty, and so under these conditions you get to know each other really well. So it was with some amusement that the lovely Administration Officer come to my office door this morning and said "look, the admin catch up is in five minutes, do you need to go to the toilet?"

My face must have been a picture of horror, before laughing out loud at such a personal question. She explained later that as we'd been together for a few days, she'd become accustomed to me dashing down the corridor with 60 seconds to spare in between meetings so she wanted to help. Which in actual fact, is really sweet and more than a little funny.

What has also become apparent over the last few days, in the deathly quiet of the building, is she can hear most of my meetings. They aren't private and I don't mind but today she decided to comment on them. But in a lovely way dear diary. And it was lovely.

She told me that from her experience of over ten years at the school, she thought I'd set a high standard in organisation and my close management and guidance to the staff during the production of next year's budget was what was needed. Also, that I'd shaken the shit out of the organisation. I was flattered. It's been a week of 8 am to 6 pm back-to-back meetings; going through things with these talented, dedicated but not always commercially aware, academics and trying to make their life easier. The conversation today did make me reflect on a description of me from a previous life.

It went like this. 'She's gonna come in, break your toys and mess your hair up; and you won't even notice!' I think that's a compliment!

So tonight, I am a little liquored up as we had R U OK day drinks and by God I needed it.

Aside from meetings about next year's budget, I spent some time in our main switch board today. I don't know why I was looking at it. I know nothing more about electricity than the currency differences between the US/Asia/UK and Aus and how that impacts my hairdryer. But I looked at it knowingly, continually nodding with (fake) understanding like I was an electrical engineer. I do know money though and I know that amid everything, bloody, else, I need a new switch and a capacity increase of 20% to accommodate a new building in the development pipeline.

But let's speak about capacity with the vaccination rates in NSW – 76.3% first dose, 43% fully vaxxed and with another stunning 1542 COVID cases today.

Right, I'm going to make some dinner before I fall off this stool in a gin-soaked heap. Until tomorrow, dear diary. Until tomorrow…

Lock-Down-Under - Day 78 - 20 years later....

Oh, dear diary.

Today is 11 September 2021.

Maybe it was because I knew it was a day of reflection, dear diary. Maybe I knew what the subject of TV documentaries would be today. Maybe I knew how twenty years ago these actions would change the world, change our attitudes and change all our lives. Just maybe I knew all that. And so maybe that's why I was awake at 3.40 this morning! After watching one of those documentaries and having a long glass of water; enough reflection, I decided. The new focus and decision was for an early smash and grab at Bunnings.

It was forecast to be a lovely day and it was time for me to sort my balcony out. I've had an umbrella stuck in the cupboard for a few years and plant pots empty for the same period. Today's the day! Pot day!

Unable to find the green wall trellis I wanted; I've managed to sort the rest. I have six pots full of plants and a nice clean balcony. All this and some washing done by 11am, so time to enjoy it.

What's not so nice today is the NSW 1599 COVID cases, nor is it lovely that it's day 78. Without any stress or mental health considerations in this statement; it's now f*cking ridiculous. I understand the bad media today regarding the Federal Health Minister not meeting Pfizer Executives last year. I suspect Government were trying to avoid allowing the Execs to behave in a manner similar to vultures picking at the carcass of a body. As that's probably the exact approach they intended! Profiteering from disaster. This wouldn't have been a charity approach; this was a mercenary approach. A country in lockdown, without a vaccine – yet. Here Australia, do we have a deal for you.

I understand the Governments rationale but I'm also a lot pissed that we don't seem to be any further forward in the last 12 months! A year ago, I asked on a FaceTube group page how folks felt about lockdown. Best thing, they said. Yeah, let's have this conversation in a year when we are still in this position; and here we bloody well are!

Back to this day, 20 years ago. On 11 September 2001, I had just moved into a new home in the Hunter Valley. I was on a tactical Air Traffic Course, and this was the last night. We had been partying! We had been partying hard, celebrating finishing a fairly intensive course with its culmination field phase. It was late into the night in Australia, when we saw the planes fly into the Towers. The whole course, or those old die-hards who were left in the bar anyway, stopped drinking.

We made coffee and knocked on the doors of the couple of our course mates that had gone to bed.

We sat down to soberly watch this tragedy unfold for the rest of the night. Speaking among ourselves and wondering what this meant for us now.

The course we had just completed was a qualifying course to deploy as a battlespace air trafficker. We all knew it was going to happen sooner than we thought. Before breakfast we had checked our equipment and packed our bags in readiness. Two of us were told later that day that we were on immediate notice to deploy. It was a strange 24 hours, and that was just the tip of the iceberg! Twenty years ago.

Anyway, back to present day. I have a clean balcony to enjoy, sun to worship and a session with my mentee to prepare for.

Then it'll be an early bed, cos did I say dear diary that I was up at 3.40am!

Until tomorrow dear diary. Until tomorrow....

Lock-Down-Under - Day 79 - And on Sunday she rested....

Well, dear diary,

I'm doing the same. Today is a day of rest for me. Yeah, apart from the 7.30 to 9.30 work catch up, so I don't hyperventilate when I open my inbox tomorrow.

Oh, and yep, that two-hour board meeting. I had to do it without the camera on! No hair and make-up needed for that as it's Sunday for the love of God. A day of rest! And that includes make-up and hair! This volunteering stuff can be a pain when the weather is glorious!

So, the rest of the day is mine! All mine. And this daily diary memoire, like me, is short but sweet!

But unlike Gladys, I'll be back tomorrow!

Oh....yeah 1262 btw.

Until tomorrow dear diary. Until tomorrow.

Lock-Down-Under - Day 80 - today I dug a hole dad!

I think that line was from The Castle, dear diary. Only I didn't dig a hole, I chain sawed down a termite damaged tree. Let me tell you how good that felt! Photo is on my website.

But I'm time poor today. My apologies.

So, NSW cases are 1257 and I need to dash to the shops cos I need a drink tonight!

Until tomorrow dear diary. Until tomorrow.....

Lock-Down-Under - Day 81 – when she's good she's very, very good, but when she's bad, she's better

Oh, dear diary,

What a quandary. It really is a mess.

This lockdown is just encouraging bad habits. I've gone back to a nightly glass of wine. I have chocolate in my house for the first time in years! Years! I even have a large Tupperware box filled with four different types of chocolate biscuits. In my defence, dear diary I do limit both the wine and the chocolate but man, it's bloody hard. I mean who doesn't want 'just one more' when there is bugger-all else to do in the dark, in the LGA, in the house....?? It's like Adam and Eve in the garden of Eden, my fridge is just tempting me. I do think I walked back up to it again though and I swear I heard it say, 'what the hell do you want now?'

If it's not the fridge I am pestering, it's the computer. An Achillies heel amidst all this is the internet shopping and that needs some significant contemplation. In addition, I know work is getting busier and it's tempting or more accurately, easier just to continue working when there is nothing else to do. In all fairness, my mind screams 'GO FOR A WALK, BITCH!' but then just another two minutes turns into two hours. Not awfully healthy to have this much screen time. To have a break, I do try to walk away from the work computer, but I think that's when the fridge looks at me frowningly. In some defence of this, I still have some of my other side hustles to look after too so that takes a little more screen time.

And that's when you see them… all the different email adverts for STUFF.

Who am I to resist, dear diary? I can't buy any more shoes as I've used up all the shoe space and more, so it's the other STUFF. I'm waiting on three parcels at the minute and the tracking is not assisted by this bloody spam we are all getting via text. I am also a little conscious that a parcel from the Candy Harlot can been seen as something very untoward. Unfortunately, though, dear diary, apart from some unsolicited emails from Donny Raymondo, some dreams of Hugh as my Bubble Buddy and a couple of calls with Hot UK Ex, my life just ain't that interesting!

Also not entirely interesting is the NSW COVID cases today 1127. Yeah, nothing else to add there today sweetheart. Nope, nuthin!

Anyway, I am going to finish work on time for once this week as I have a glass of wine and a chocolate biscuit with my name all over it. '

Until tomorrow, dear diary. Until tomorrow…..

Lock-Down-Under - Day 82 – oh, bring on the Welsh Guards

Oh, dear diary,

I can't recall what mischief and shenanigans we were up to at the time. But it would have been fun. Oh yes indeed, it would have been fun.

In a galaxy and time far, far away, it could have been an Army/Navy rugby match. It could have been a night out in Shawbury. Maybe Yeovilton. Or potentially Cyprus. I cannot recall the location, but at one stage a hilarious, very tipsy friend uttered loudly 'Bring on the Welsh Guards' in a very saucy manner.

I'd love to recall what prompted those excited utterances, but it's completely slipped my mind with the ravages of time. The whole phrase still comes to mind with extreme regularity, and it always makes me smile. And so it was, dear diary, when I saw this post on our apartment complex FaceTube page.

> So Police and Army here doing
> compliance checks on units.
>
> Wow. Bit nerve wracking

👍 Like   💬 Comment   ⊘ Send

I don't know what made me look at FaceTube in the middle of the day, but it caused my heart to pound fast. Not with the anxiety shown by my neighbour but because I was wearing my cat-sucked look fisherman's sweater, grubby jeans that are too big and some Ugg boots. My face was naked, hair in a ponytail and I was wearing glasses. In summary, I could be described as a Pig in Knickers! Not fit for man nor beast, so to speak. I had work to do.

Twenty minutes later, the girls were shoved into a bra for the first time in a while, make-up on, nice black t-shirt and my wedge, Havianna flipflops. I was ready for any Welsh Guard-like man that tapped on my door. Fortune favours the brave? Well, they better gird their loins and get ready if they knock on my door. There would be screams reverberating around the complex "LET ME OUT"

Alas, no home delivery of Beef Cake for me. But I was ready dear diary, I really was. God help any Welsh Guard had he darkened my door.

But speaking of bad luck and her indoors. Gladys posted today that 80% of NSW residents aged 16 and over have had their first vaccination.

A more comprehensive report is as follows: 276,176 doses were administered on 13 September, which was the latest reporting period. Australia wide 14,120,010 people have had their first dose, which equates to 55.14% of the total population or 68.48% of 16+ and 8,915,972 are fully vaccinated. This being 34.71% of all Australians, 43.24% of 16+.

NSW is expected to hit 80% first-dose vaccination coverage in people aged 16 and over today.

That's the vaccination rollout figures but the downside is the NSW COVID cases today were still a wild 1259. Yeah, getting used to it, we're going to see these figures for a while.

Anyway, back to work for a clean-up of final work and with a nice glass of red as an incentive.

Until tomorrow, dear diary. Until tomorrow......

Lock-Down-Under - Day 83 – sometimes you have to live with it before you know you like it

Oh, dear diary,

It's been a busy day, and I haven't stopped.

No lunch, no breakfast, no nibbles, no chocolate, just a bad habit of a coffee and a bit better habit of herbal tea. It's just been an extraordinarily busy time with a presentation to a bunch of accountants in the middle of the day. Luckily it was over Zoom so I couldn't see their grey socks and woollen cardigans.

But now? Now I need to go and pick up the slab of Negroni Spritzer that are on sale – scream. Not a little four pack for me today. This is the mother-load of offers and six times the joy.

However, I did take a few minutes to move my study around. It's been a few months since the last move and sometimes you need to let things settle, assess, consider a little more and then decide before any upheaval. The study arrangement wasn't efficient nor was it tidy or aesthetically pleasing. Therefore, a move of the printer, my funky but OCD tidy filing tray and, because I'm retro, my stereo. Yep, I'm a vinyl and CD girl still and completely love it.

Strangely I learned the same lesson with hubby number two. We spent so much time apart that it was when we actually started living together that we realised we didn't like it. Ah if only I'd picked that lesson up after number one. But there you go!

Also disappointing in numbers is NSW COVID cases today, 1352. I bloody give in. I really give in. But I do have a tidy study!

Sigh *puts on shoes and heads out to pick up the booz*

Until tomorrow, dear diary. Until tomorrow….

Lock-Down-Under - Day 84 – there's a couple of villages missing theirs…

Oh, dear diary,

For the love of the wee man, what can we say dear diary?

The coppers and the army were here a few days ago and judging by the latest message on social media, advertising for a World Wide Rally for Freedom, we may see them again tomorrow. It so happens that for the Sydney Rally, the location is my beautiful freedom location, Sydney Park.

I did, however, love how our local FaceTube pages have risen to the occasion and are giving us a warning that the rally is on, and to stay away. In fact, I haven't seen one comment of actual support for the gathering anywhere in the multiple 100s of responses advising us to "Keep Away from Sydney Park"

> I'm up for meeting them at the train station and giving them a slap. A proper erko welcome
>
> 9h   Like   Reply   8

This was met with an even better response.
'I hope it starts hailing!'
'Hailing brick, preferably!'

On the bright side, I bet there will be some good-looking coppers over there. Maybe one of two strong blokes and maybe even one or two will have a passing resemblance to Hugh Jackman. Okay, note to self. Start drinking at breakfast tomorrow morning and by the time 12 o clock comes, they'll all look like Hugh Jackman.

Hic "No, sorry Officer. You aren't quite good looking enough for me!" said no tipsy single blonde heroine ever.

Well, I know you don't read this for my remarkably funny repartee and banter. I know the readers want the scores on the doors. Oh yes, they do dear diary.

Well NSW COVID cases today were 1284. I actually think that's made-up shit figures as that's a number I recognise from a previous report. Or maybe this has just been going on too long. The bright side is NSW is over 50% double dose vaccinations and they are starting an isolation at home trial, instead of locked in a hotel.

Oh, gentlemen start your engines. Freedom is looking a lot closer.

Anyway, I have a case of Negroni Spritzer to make a dent in. So, until tomorrow, dear dairy. Until tomorrow…..

Lock-Down-Under - Day 85 – beating the rain and the riot

Oh, dear diary,

My day didn't go as planned. Not as planned. Not at all.

I was all in for a long lie. I wanted to sleep longer than 5am. Longer than 6am. Longer than 7am. In preparation for Operation Rip Van Winton, I had even pulled down the black out blind in my room. I closed the other doors to block out the morning light. I was set, I was so so set. It was even like someone was singing "I'm gonna have a good night" in the background. Yep, I was very ready.

Yeah, no joy. It was a little disappointing that I was watching TV at 3.30 am. After a few more restless hours it all over. By 7am and I was up and trying to get ready. Today was going to be a gentle little 8-10km walk.

Now that would have been easy if not for one of the obstacles in the way. This morning being my bloody contact lenses. I've been wearing these slippery little suckers for 20 years; since I was a wee itsy-bitsy bairn, clearly, and after the first two days found them simple to use.

Not. Bloody. Today. The left one was in and out six times before I finally got it settled; this was almost forty minutes later. It was about 8.30 before I started out on my trek.

To add insult to injury, those that read the Day 84 post, you'll know there's a demonstration planned about 50m from my home today. Sydney Park was identified as the venue for World Freedom Rally and with that comes a lot of police. A lot of police. They were stationed at every rail station, most major road intersections and roaming the streets. It was beefcake smorgasbord day to be sure but felt a little uncomfortable and oppressive at the same time. And I say this having been bloody locked up for twelve weeks.

But some of the better views around the 'hood is the street art on the homes along my walking circuits. It's become quite the trend in Inner West to have the side of your house painted up. It's pretty nice stuff.

Not so lovely are the lunatics without masks doing all the protesting. Nor are the NSW COVID cases today of 133, or the fact it started raining halfway round.

But I don't care now as I have a few movies to watch. 85% of that slab of Negroni Spritzer and some chocolate to keep me warm this afternoon. Time to relax and breathe.

Until tomorrow, dear diary. Until tomorrow…..

Lock-Down-Under - Day 86 - stupid is as stupid does

Oh, dear diary,

There's one born every minute and I think I saw a few minutes' worth whilst walking yesterday.

Some of the cute little streets with their funky "street art" and narrow roads are divine. I wouldn't want to park there but they're aesthetically pleasing. Then there are the challenges. Of course there are challenges! There are always challenges. Yesterday it was a big lorry that was challenged! Or more specifically, the crew.

Now it's problematic for bigger vehicles to move down these streets anyway, because the gap between the cars alone makes it tight. Gotta be a careful driver. But let's add in low hanging cables. Cables that are lower than the roof of the vehicle. What does one do?

Well, I'm used to planning stuff from a military perspective and time spent on reconnaissance is never wasted. But these guys are not close to the military, that's for certain. If they were, they would have scoped out the low hanging cables by maybe walking along the street, knowing the height of the vehicle, maybe some online research and entered the street in a manner to remain clear.

Did they do that? Oh no, dear diary, no they didn't. They reached for the trusty broomstick, much like my mothers, but instead of using it as a mode of transport, they used it to try to rearrange the power cables and physically lift them over the roof of the lorry. Power cables. Live power cables. At least it was a wooden broom and not a metal brush pole; or was it?

Noting that they were standing on the back tail-lift for height, presumably it was only to lift it over the back lip of the truck. The plan then is that they would then drive forward letting the cable drag along the roof and hope it doesn't snag on anything. I've always though hope is the best course of action when dealing with high voltage cables.

Darwin Award nominations 2022 open yet??

I had to walk away. The Australian WHS legislation is pretty severe for people who just stand by and watch bad shit happen! Best not to watch. Besides none of them looked very clean, or like Hugh Jackman (whom I'd like dirty!) so absolutely no danger of me providing mouth to mouth if shit got real.

Talking about real. NSW COVID cases today were 1083 which is a little better, and now all LGAs can indulge in picnics. Excellent; I just need 5 friends in my LGA! Yeah, there's the limitation!

Anyway, I have some red wine open, and it is nearly 3pm, so until tomorrow dear diary. Until tomorrow....

Lock-Down-Under - Day 87 – walking into wonderful

Oh, dear diary,

What a delight. An absolute delight.

I have lived in this apartment for six years and have never seen this. It was pretty nice, and I don't think the image I could take on my phone does it justice. Throwing off the shackles of looking after a large house as a single girl, I bought this apartment. It's not in the CBD but in the trendy Inner West of Sydney. It's about 2km from the CBD and close to everything. The views of the city are lovely, but I've never seen it this spectacular. And there's reasons for that.

My lovely apartment has sun streaming through the windows from dawn until dusk. Well on sunny days that happens. The living room windows that allow access out to the balcony are north facing and it's perfect. In the evening the sun moves onto the west walls, and it keeps the living room cooler in the evenings in summer. As I am OCD, I normally have a sunshade blind down when I'm not in the room to protect the floor and the furniture. Friday was going to be rainy and cloudy, so I went to work and the blind was raised. No big issue. I also didn't get home until about 6.30 pm; so it was dark.

Well dear diary it feels like a perfect storm, or for those familiar with the Reason Model for accidents, I missed some other steps in my OCD process and the Reason Model Cheese Holes lined up. When I drive into the car park and start to lose phone signal, I normally shout/scream/impersonate a fishwife towards the phone and instruct Google to "turn on the kitchen lights." I didn't do this either and so my apartment was pitch black. Then I opened the door, and a magnificent sight greeted me.

The view was a beautifully lit city with Barangaroo as the prominent star in the middle. Barangaroo is a newly developed part of Sydney from an old wharf area and very trendy. There is a new casino that is having some licencing issues, but that's another story. I loved the view from the door, the vibrant and bright city, so stunning through the darkness of my apartment. It reminded me why I live here and why I bought this place. Having lived in country towns all my life, I am not yet fed up with the city life and or its views.

Unfortunately, the city is also predominantly where the virus is living, but a little bit of good news is that NSW COVID cases today dropped below 1000 for the first time in a month. With a slightly better 935, I hope it continues to drop.

Anyway, with wishful thinking and a positive attitude I go forth.

Until tomorrow, dear diary. Until tomorrow....

Lock-Down-Under - Day 88 – two fat ladies

Oh, dear diary,

How I miss a bit of Tranny bingo.

I don't think this was the Tranny bingo wording for 88 but who cares? I think that an aesthetically good-looking number. Is it just me? Or is it that I started on the sauce too early?

Ironically as lovely numbers go todays NSW COVID cases are back up again to 1022.

Maybe it's because I think I need a nice gin. Maybe I've spent too long staring at a screen today. Regardless of any maybes, I certainly have a little writers block. Who would ever have thought they'd hear me say that? The woman who has Jane Austin in fear of her skills. Or I would have if she were still alive. Yep she'd be shitting herself at my literature writing abilities!

For a bit of headspace, I am going for a walk. I am going to enjoy the fresh air and feel the wind in my hair and anywhere else I want to. Without getting arrested or causing children to run screaming in fear, obviously.

Until tomorrow dear diary. Until tomorrow.....

Lock-Down-Under - Day 89 - out of the mouths of electronic devices

So dear diary,

I think there's an argument to be had.

The argument being that these Google and Alexa gadgets are continually listening to us. By jove, I think it's right dear diary: I really think they are.

My bedroom device is imaginatively called The Penthouse Bedroom. So, when I gave it my best fishwife squawk last night to turn off the lights, the bloody thing responded: -

"I'm sorry. Something has gone wrong with the Penthouse Bedroom!" Ain't that the bloody truth!?

On reflection, maybe it's preparing for tomorrow. Tomorrow will see a mid-week sleep in and general indulgent morning relaxation.

Why?

Because tomorrow is my birthday. I'm thinking of pulling a sickie, having breakfast in bed, alone as Hugh was strangely unavailable! Then embarking on a walk up to Darling Harbour and some selfish, fresh air with a side helping of peace and quiet. No meetings. No Zoom. No calls. No e-mail. No stress. No work. This healthy morning may well be followed by bubbles and a nice steak.

My friends may pay their individual homages to me throughout the day, at my convenience! One amazing friend, she of the Welsh Guards fame, has remembered this day, every year for the 23 years I have been here in Australia. And despite me being the bitch that forgets birthdays, she sends me a great card, every year. I love you, Ali!

It's not all about me though, NSW COVID cases today were 1035. Meanwhile in Melbourne, more protesters have taken to the streets and the city has protested by producing an earthquake! No shit. A little overkill Melbourne, but whatever it takes.

On the vaccine front, 321,168 doses were administered nationwide on 20 September. 15,002,990 people have had at least one dose which equates to 59.45% of the total population or 72.76% of 16+ and 9,842,760 are fully vaccinated. This is 38.32% of all Australians, 47.73% of 16+. In NSW, 83.02% of 16+ have had at least one dose and 54.2% have had two.

Also, from Lee's house of useless knowledge, on today 22 Sep, it's 100 days to New Year's Eve.

Today is the day I traditionally start 100 Days of Happiness! It was something I started a few years ago and it's a silly little of habit of having to post the happiest thing that has happened to you that day. This may sound a little silly, but it subconsciously forces you to look for the bright part of your whole day and everything that happens in it. It's a lovely way to change your thinking. Truly lovely. However, I think there is enough being posted on FaceTube at the minute, including my daily diary. Besides, I do believe trying to find happiness when you're a prisoner in your own home is asking a little too much. Surely this is enough.

So, until tomorrow dear diary when it's a big Happy Birthday to me...... Until tomorrow Birthday Girl....

Lock-Down-Under - Day 90 – the first casualty of war is the plans

So dear diary,

The Birthday Girl had a day planned. Oh, did she ever have a day planned. And bloody work wasn't part of it. No siree, no it wasn't.

My day involved a champagne breakfast (in bed alone admittedly), a walk around this beautiful city, maybe a late afternoon sub-picnic in the park with wine, steak and salad for dinner and certainly, certainly no work.

Well, all those plans have disappeared in the last 24 hours. Disappeared is maybe an understatement. They have more accurately been the subject of a nuclear detonation. So now today involves meetings at 8.30, 9, 11, 2 and 3.30. I think it's a big no to the steak and salad I planned for dinner, I'm picking up a pizza for dinner. Then the champagne, planned optimistically for breakfast is going to get a spanking for dinner.

On the bright side, flexibility in the plans was also a lesson from my Defence days. Well dear diary, not quite that phrase; it was always "flexibility is the key to air supremacy" but I'm adapting it to suit my needs today. My birthday morning has started with three phone calls, two cups of coffee in bed and the last few remaining, highly coveted chocolate 'Twix pods' that originally assisted my budget meeting yesterday. We need to take hold of those little pleasures when we get them.

Something not so pleasurable is the NSW COVID cases today was again a stunning 1063. Still over that 1000, but what can we expect with absolutely no discipline.

But an update on vaccines. Well 332,010 doses were administered nationwide on 21 September. This means that15,140,888 people have had at least one dose; 60.1% of the total population or 73.43% of 16+ and 10,006,715 are fully vaccinated or 38.96% of all Australians, 48.53% of 16+.

In NSW, 83.6% of 16+ have had at least one dose and 55.5% have had two.

From my thinking if the doses are three or four weeks apart, then Gladys is on track for 26 October opening and I for one can't wait.

My trip to Darwin was cancelled.

My trip to Coolangatta was cancelled.

My trip to Tassie is still on for November.

Fingers crossed. But I haven't seen The Oatmeal Savage and my dad for nearly two years now... time is up!

Anyway, I still have three meetings ahead and a bottle of bubbles with my name on it. In fact, I am sure it says, "come and get me Birthday Girl" Oh how I wish those words were from Hugh Jackman! Maybe I speak of him too often, judging by some of the birthday messages.

Until tomorrow, dear diary. Until tomorrow......

Lock-Down-Under - Day 91 – Oh good grief. I have a wheelbarrow full of gold and now I have to push it ALL the way to the bank

Well, dear diary,

I was exhausted yesterday.

Exhausted, truly pooped, I tell you and it wasn't work. It wasn't the 6.30 start on the computer from the comfort of my king size bed with its soft sheets and blankets that make me go, ahhhhh. Oh no, the two coffees and Twix pods overcame any sleepiness that may have eventuated by an early rise and a grab of the computer more than overcame that. In fact, that injection of caffeine had me running hot all day. Quite the Supercharged Blonde. More than any mortal man can handle. But Hugh is more than a mere man! No, no, it wasn't work that fair tuckered me out yesterday. It was the talking!

Okay, I can see the eyerolls! Stop it right now.

I know I'm a talker. You all know I'm a talker.

I love it.

I mean who doesn't love a good gossip?

That's me. I lean right into any and all conversations. But on my 10th or so call by midday, well, I was exhausted. When the final call appeared at 8.30pm there was that moment of temptation to let it go to the keeper. No, couldn't do it. I've always considered myself blessed to have the very bestest of friends, so no way does a phone go unanswered to one of them. That's not what friends do. Friends talk. Friends laugh. Friends grab lunch. Friends share booze. They share the highs and lows. That's what friends do. I love my friends.

One communication yesterday reminded me of another, quite colourful actor friend in the US.

A previous ex-boyfriend was nicknamed Scruffy the Love Rat, and despite it now being over ten years since we went out, he emailed to wish me a Happy Birthday.

All very lovely certainly, but the thing that made me laugh yesterday, and every time, was the amendment to the name given to Scruffy by my US friend. I think she felt that the four names were overkill and pointedly renamed him Rat Bastard. A tad harsh perhaps? But amusing, nonetheless. Especially in these circumstances.

Also more than a tad harsh is the relentless daily lack of reduction in NSW COVID cases. Today was 1043. I will submit that the positive aspect is that it's not 2000, or 3000, or worse. Australia is also vaccinating one million people every 3 days, so let's get this bloody country open soon!

Finally, thanks to you all for all the birthday wishes. and for the pictures of Hugh... He finally knows I exist he sent me a Happy Birthday signed picture! Sigh, I think it came from someone else but, one can always dream.

Due to extreme exhaustion, there will be no drive through of the gin place tonight. That's tomorrow's essential supply run.

So, until tomorrow, dear diary. Until tomorrow.

Lock-Down-Under - Day 92 – yeah though I walk into the valley of the shadow of death

Oh, dear diary,

You may think this is a little bit dramatic. But hear me out!

When I tell you what I did this morning, I think you'll agree I put myself in the firing line. Yep, I put myself into danger. Danger of the gravest variety. This isn't the first time this situation has occurred. In fact, the last time my parents were with me, and my poor Mum also nearly died. This isn't the time to make jokes about the demise of The Oatmeal Savage. I hope that old cow lives forever! I mean who will do my ironing and bathroom cleaning if she can't visit again! Furthermore, if I ever buy another house with a pool, I'll certainly need Eduardo the Pool Boy who always comes to visit with her and is affectionately known as Dad.

No, this morning is domestic danger and threat. Let me explain dear diary.

I love Aldi. My friends know that similar to my love of talking, Hugh, shoes, Hugh and gin, my love of Aldi and the ability to buy a fridge and ski clothes when doing your weekly shopping has no limits. Stuff that you realistically don't need and maybe won't ever need, but in that one frenzied moment you feel your life wouldn't be complete without. The danger lies when they have something on their twice weekly special buys that attracts, well, everyone; you take your life in your own hands when trying to get your desired share.

This morning, I woke with a panic at 8.05 and knew that if I was going to make the opening at 8.30, I would have to shake some white Scottish ass. I made it at 8.40 and went straight to the new Saturday buys where all the solar and smart lighting was displayed. I wanted those solar festoon lights for my balcony and by God I was going to get them.

On entering today's adventure, I recalled the not so fond memories of this type of expedition previously when I'd witnessed people commando crawling under the roller doors as they were being raised. I think that was for Dyson Vacuums. There was also the near-death experience for my beloved Oatmeal Savage. When she was trying to pick up something or other, probably for me, some goat of a bloke nearly decapitated her during a testosterone filled show of brute strength and ignorance. In the middle of the packed store be proceeded to swing a wine fridge up and over his shoulder, presumably to carry his 'kill' to the checkout! Mum look positively afraid, as the box at full pelt missed her by millimetres, and I've never, ever, seen anything scare that bitch.

The mission today, operation Lumiere was a success. The lights were successfully acquired with only one tiny encounter and some minor fastest-fingers-first grabbing with another woman over one of the last two boxes! Yeah, she wanted two and I wanted one. Victory is mine. The solar panel is now charging in readiness of the festoon of LED globes later tonight. That balcony is gonna look flasher than a rat with a gold tooth!

Speaking about dangerous pursuits – I saw an advert on our local FaceTube page the other day casting for First Dates Australia. Should I or shouldn't I? Oh, hell, yes. Who wouldn't want a first date with this Little Blonde Heroine? I mean seriously! The world needs to experience this amazing chick. Doesn't it?

Speaking about serious, NSW COVID cases today was 1007. But Freedom Day is 11 Oct; another day closer. Just over two weeks in fact.

Right though, now I may have a First Dates bio application to write, TV to watch, gin to drink. Okay so it's only 11am but it's a Saturday so hear me out!

Until tomorrow dear diary. Until tomorrow....

Lock-Down-Under - Day 93 - memories of childhood past

Oh, dear diary,

It's got to the last straw. The very last straw.

I couldn't look at my feet any longer. One further glance downwards and I was going to take to my toes with a large carving knife. I couldn't bear it. No more. The positive side though is considering the additional COVID kilograms, I guess I'm lucky I can actually see my bloody feet.

There I was, resigned to the task ahead. It was always going to be unpleasant, but it was now or never, only without Elvis. White peely-wally, Scottish skin encased in a towel, hunting for nail polish remover and I knew that to remove the residual of that long ago pedicure polish, I was going to need the high voltage stuff avec acetone! Yep, the heavy-duty paint stripper.

Then I would need to pick the colour! It needed to be a bold one, because it needed to cover the remnants of the polish I couldn't get off! I love a good back up plan.

Now I recall a line from a film that you don't actually need a professional pedicure. No, all you need is regular walks on the beach and a steady hand. Geez, with this lockdown, I think I need an industrial sander. And a steady hand? Well, after two coffees this morning that ain't looking so positive either. Maybe if I had given up the coffee and wine a few days prior this would have gone a little more smoothly.

This whole situation was a reminder of my time coming out of Afghanistan. Feet clad in boots for months on end and unloved, my lovely friend Mick J took me out for a luxury treat when I hit UAE! In an amazing upmarket salon, in one of the upmarket shopping centres, it was beautiful, clean, serene and I took in my manky hooves! The lovely ladies in Dubai looked down on my not-so-cute tootsies with a horrified face and without even consulting me, they reached for the paraffin treatment!

Today, I gave it my best shot with the orange OPI polish.

Afterwards, when I saw orange dots on both my ankle and jeans, in addition to most of my big toe, all off the nail, it reminded me of Mr Blobby. It made me laugh in reflection, of its antics all those years ago. Who didn't love that kids Saturday Show; you know, that one that made such an impact that I've forgotten the name of it! With that Noel bloke; him with the beard and the high-pitched giggle!

Another thing I'm going to forget in a hurry is the NSW COVID cases today 961. Not great but heading in the good direction.

Freedom Day reminder. It's planned for 11 Oct. Two weeks, boys and girls, two weeks. Not long now. So, until tomorrow when it's another day closer dear diary. Until tomorrow.....

P.S. Images on the website, but I think one of those pictures of Mr B looks a bit rude!

Lock-Down-Under - Day 94 – my sentiments exactly

Ah dear diary,

Just a quick run-down the motorway today and into work.

There is certain mandatory reporting in this job that need to be done on computer screens the size of a cinema. Today, that's absolutely what I needed. I needed full size cinema scope for the statistics to be fed into the abyss of the Department of Education system today. Four spreadsheets, two people, two computer programs and three hours of work but there we are. Again, a successful plan executed. Then a quick dash home after lunch because the Board meeting starts at 4pm and I have multiple hours of Zoom meetings beforehand.

However, a lovely thing happened the other day. One of the staff gave me a great little gift. It was an awesome little keyring and sometimes I think it suited my attitude entirely. It said 'A wise woman once said, Fuck this Shit. And she lived happily ever after.' It did make me think what type of behaviour I portrayed. What could I do but laugh and nod when I saw it.

I told the guys about the gift at our Monday morning get together. This was when my team gave me the not-so-anonymous 360-degree feedback. They thought my attitude to what was important, and what wasn't, was refreshing and liked the fact that I provided strong leadership and guidance and also that I laughed a lot. Laughter which can generally be heard all over the building. One of the finance team then admitted to having a recording of my laughter as the ringtone for my number on her phone. She then proceeded to demonstrate the sound clip! This in turn had us all in fits and altogether, it was a pretty nice way to start the day.

Then maybe a little better is the fact that NSW COVID cases were 787. Its dropping – yippee!!! Let's get this done and get out of here! Road map to freedom on 11 October was specified today by the Premier.

More information on vaccines too. 219,373 doses were administered nationwide on 25 September. Now 15,633,342 people have had at least one dose, equating to 62.46% of the total population or 75.82% of 16+. 10,616,323 are fully vaccinated equalling 41.33% of all Australians, 51.49% of 16+. In NSW, 85.5% of 16+ have had at least one dose and 60.1% have had two. The light is no longer an oncoming train.

Okay, lunch time is over, and I need to start preparing for the afternoon.

Until tomorrow, dear diary. Until tomorrow….

Lock-Down-Under - Day 95 – "tell 'im he's dreaming"

Oh, dear diary,

For those who have watched that Australian icon movie The Castle, they'll recognise that phrase.

Not only will they recognise it but then thoughts will enter their heads of other legendary sayings including:
- Bonnie Doon
- Feeling the Serenity
- That's our Steve, he's the ideas man.

And the most classic of all classics.

- That's going straight to the poolroom.

But it's the "tell him he's dreaming" phrase that came to mind last night when I saw how I could part with $2200. I could spend it on Chanel shoes. Not bloody likely.

I have grown to love this ridiculous FaceTube page where people are now clearly trying to redeem the financial outlay of COVID impulse spending and most definitely not selling them. In this case, it's a set of very naff 'dad' sandals without the obligatory grey socks that would normally accompany such footwear! Once again, it's not the goods being sold that is the most amusing, it's the comments that amuse the hell out of me. Like the $50 Chanel candles on offer a few weeks ago, the comments were swift and merciless. My personal favourite? I'd be less embarrassed if someone saw me licking the seat of a festival toilet wearing Crocs than be seen with these!

Also amusing is the announcement today that our international borders are opening up and it's combined with home isolation when returning! About bloody time Yeah, Patsy, I am coming home!

Unfortunately, the mess that started all this continues with NSW COVID cases today still coming in at an unfortunate 863. However, it's from over 132,000 tests.

I'm now thinking of looking for my copy of The Castle; that may be tonight's adventure.

Until tomorrow, dear diary. Until tomorrow….

Lock-Down-Under - Day 96 – priorities…priorities….

Yeah, dear diary,

That's it completely. I have finally lost all control of impulses and sense.

I am done. I cancelled the 8.30 staff meeting this morning; justifying it to myself that 75% of my staff are on leave as it's school holidays. I persuaded myself that the five or so senior staff that would have been at the meeting will still be okay for a day. Fortunately, I will see three of them all day tomorrow and I'll commit to calling the other two. Which I did.

But why? Yeah, and here is why I think I have lost all my marbles dear diary.

It was because of a wall screen Zen-design planter from Aldi. Aldi opens at 8.30 and I knew it was going to be the usual mosh pit, so I needed a prompt attack. It's a lovely planter and is going to look spiffing with the green wall and solar fairy lights that are this weekends frenzied campaign plan. I am so much all about making this balcony look preddy!

I had a good, if a somewhat wacky plan. As always, the first casualty of war is the plans. There was a delay in delivery. The delay, which I only now know is 1pm. Sympathy should be extended to the 300 heads I trampled on today in a non-socially distanced COVID way; as it was all in vain.

However, back to my amazing staff. When I mentioned my dilemma, in response to why I started work at 6am, they all pitched in to help. One is roaming the isles of Bankstown Airport Aldi, another will be at Rhodes Shopping Centre Aldi during lunch time as they were delivered at 11am and she wants one too now. Success.

But not so preddy or successful is the NSW COVID cases today which I think are in error. 863. Recognise that numero? Yep, that was yesterdays too.

But dear diary, let's not dwell on that.

International travel is set to resume!!

Well, at least partly, once the national vaccination rate passes 80 per cent.

In preparation for this, the federal government will begin issuing international vaccination certificates from Friday. Oh halle-bloody-luiah. I have a note in my work diary to do this on Friday.

The scores on the doors to this destination. First dose is 63.34% of the total population or 76.68% of 16+ and fully vaccinated 42.2% of all Australians or 52.57% of 16+. In NSW, 86.2% of 16+ have had at least one dose and 61.7% have had two.

Okay four hours of budget and Western Sydney International Airport airspace meetings for me this afternoon.

Until tomorrow, dear diary. Until tomorrow....

Lock-Down-Under - Day 97 - does the mind see what it wants to see?

Oh, dear diary,

Wasn't yesterday such a hilarious day?

Yes, it was. Or so I think.

The Planter Purchase story is the gift that keeps giving. During the purchase, the wonderful Belinda began to send pictures of all other things on offer in an effort to amuse and to tempt this locked up babe. Did I need a caravan cover? Did I need a petrol can with a retractable spout? Did I need a hot dog maker? And so began the arrival of all these images.

Now here is where the wheels fell off. Before I knew it was a hot dog maker, one glance at this specific image had me gasping! "What the actual hell?? She's sent me a picture of a willy!" It took about 5-8 seconds before I realised this was the hot dog maker. And that's when the giggling started. This was a story I had to share....

We thought this was the end of planter-gate saga but apparently not. In making the payment to Bel, I managed to add an extra 0. Effectively, between payment and refund, over $1900 has changed hands today.

But speaking of excessive numbers, today's NSW COVID cases were 941. Yep, some increases again. Smaller though, small mercies. In writing this I can't believe I think 941 is a small mercy when we started over 12 weeks ago with less than 20 infections. I know. I know.

I have no more words today, more tomorrow! Until tomorrow, dear diary. Until tomorrow....

Lock-Down-Under - Day 98 – usurped by, well, everything

Oh, dear diary,

It doesn't matter what I say today it'll get lost in the noise.

That noise being an announcement:
- International flights reopening in NSW in November
- Seven days home quarantine available
- Federal cabinet re-shuffle
- NSW Premier has resigned for dating a Darryl - who hasn't dated a Darryl?

NSW COVID cases today were 864.

Until tomorrow, dear diary when I will have tales of planter box building, fights to get the green wall, a venture to Bunnings and whatever else amuses me in the next 24 hours. So, until then….

Lock-Down-Under - Day 99 - Oh put it away love. You're not impressing anyone with that....

Oh, dear diary,

Really? I mean seriously!

Some weeks you take your life in your own hands when venturing into the Aldi special buy realm, but not this morning seemingly! I wanted the next missing piece of the puzzle.... green wall! It comes in Laurel and Ivy patterns, and I wanted to go see which one I wanted.

So always observing the sacrosanct of "clean sheet Saturday " rules, I managed to jam the sheets into the washer and out the door at 8am for the war against my shopping opponents!

Well, heavens to Murgatroyd, quelle surprisè, plenty left and no fights. In fact, it was a disappointingly no news shop and quickly back home. This meant dear diary, there was time aplenty to clean the apartment and build the planter boxes. Yeah, that wasn't going to be a quick job! It was like these bad boys were IKEA patented! 7 slabs of metal and about 3000 nuts and screws. Surprisingly, whilst it was a long job, it wasn't the part of the day that may have caused a requirement for a few months in therapy.

This was. I live in an apartment complex. Moved from a large house into this joint 6 years ago. And I love it. In general, I love it.

In the complex, there is a magnificent Triumph, heavy on the chrome, motorcycle that's always parked by the lift and over the last few days, the attractive owner has been working on it. Look he's no Hugh, but he's got a bit of game! Unfortunately, this morning as I approached the lift with all my shopping and green wall, I was greeted by Mr Not-Hugh crouching down beside his bike and a very large exposed hairy arse crack! It was awful, huge and hairy; did I say it was huge. It was quite simply offensive to my delicate eyes and sensibilities! I mean hasn't he heard of wax? This was a bear in pants.

Now I've heard about phrases like "excited utterance" and "inside voice" so it was a slant on them both during this trauma that caused me to exclaim humorously "Oh ffs, that ain't a pretty sight luv!" Not-Hugh turned around, and I was forced to nervously explain to a bloke with a wrench the observation of over 50% of his gorilla resembling arse!

Whilst giggling in the same nervous manner, and trying to disappear into the floor, I nearly broke my finger pressing madly at the lift button. Praying. Praying. Praying for the lift doors to open and allow me to disappear into the 1970 porn resembling walnut walled abyss of the freedom elevator to the 6th floor! Damn those excited utterances!

Anyway a few hours later my new feature wall was 50% complete. Planters constructed. Green wall hung, thanks to my new drill! Now just some solar fairy lights and somewhere to move the umbrella are all that is outstanding.

Not outstanding was the 813 COVID cases today, but better than 1400.

Anyway, all good here after the Planter-gate journey. Until tomorrow dear diary. Until tomorrow....

Lock-Down-Under - Day 100 – oh, hello again Hugh.

Well, thanks for the journey, Centurion. One hundred days not years but you got that didn't you?

Oh, dear diary,

This is astounding.

100 days ago, I was sent home and laughingly informed that I couldn't come into work the next day. It was a Thursday, and I was miffed. I don't enjoy working from home. I don't enjoy work encroaching on my home. I don't want to walk to the office via the McKitchen for a McWinton before walking the three meters back to the home office.

I want to go to work. I like the travel to and from work. I like to get mentally set and ready on the way there and to decompress on the way home.

To add insult to injury, the LGA that was being locked in was City of Sydney, which I officially live in, by the amazing distance of little more than one metre. One bloody metre. Oh, I was pissed. I was resentful. I was mad. I didn't want to work from home. I didn't want an official home office. I want an area with more than a little bit of a desk; an where I can sit in comfort with my computer and printer. And by one lousy metre.

Yeah, that restriction quickly spread to other LGAs and very soon it wasn't just mine. It just so happened that I was trapped in the Playgirl Penthouse. I know what it's like to be trapped in one place for months on end, so I knew what I was going to think and feel. It's a strange thing to stay in one place for months at a time. It can affect you in many ways, weight, sleep and mental health. Only time will tell about the effects on the world as a result of these lock downs. Last year we heard domestic violence was up. Will long term mental health be affected? Will we see a lot of early retirements because we have gotten used to our sofa, our slippers, our home comforts? Yep, time will tell.

It has been a strange, but quick, 100 days for me. It's been trips for injections. It's been reuniting with Hot UK Ex. It's been strange emails from strangers called Jonny Love and Donald Raymondo. It's been painting walls. It's been jigsaws. It's been walking in the park. It's been a great deal of cooking. It's been reuniting with my love of wine. It's been Zoom chats with friends. It's been weekly trips to the booz shop! And it's been screen time galore. I'm getting over my hatred of working from home and finding joy in the little things. Things that are going to be more precious when we get released in 9 days.

I also feel like I have spent 100 days hunting for Hugh. Imagine my delight when I saw an image pop up on FaceTube last night. We appear to be FaceTube buddies. I don't know how he found me. Maybe those waves of longing have travelled the miles and subconsciously he knew his fate was waiting on him in the form of a small Rubenesque blonde, a fun-loving bundle of mischief. I get that it's only social media stalking and word recognition but who am I to look this gift horse in the mouth.

I wrote that day back in 2021. I am also thinking of expanding and publishing these posts. I've always wanted to write and have a lot of tales from this weird old life that I have lived. Maybe it's time. It may not come to anything, but I've always had a lot to say so why stop now? And I think I'm going to want to look back on this time in years to come. I'm thinking of calling it; One hundred days of hunting Hugh! What do you think?

Anyway, NSW COVID cases today were a heartening 667. The figures are heading in the right direction. Let's hope they stay that way.

Not as amusing, inflammatory, rude or sarcastic as usual; I know that. Today was a bit of reflection and there's always tomorrow for the rest. However, thanks to you who have taken this weird journey with me.

So, until tomorrow dear diary. Until tomorrow…

The final days of lockdown

Lock-Down-Under - Day 101 – what the actual.....??

Oh, dear diary,

I planned to stop writing to you at day 100 but COVID hasn't stopped yet, so why should I?

I mean dear diary, there must be some fun yet to be had. Surely there are things left to mock? And here it is… the FaceTube page that keeps on giving. I was a little amused at an attractive little size 10/12 red lace and black leather ensemble that was recently offered for sale. I was going to say I was shocked and stunned but I've read 50 Shades and I've read the even better Masters Thesis on BDSM and legal areas of consent written by a very talented friend, so I wasn't awfully shocked.

Nope dear diary, I was amused, and I wondered if this was a joke. I also wondered how long on a stiff diet it would take me to fit my COVID enhanced arse into it. Which is probably the biggest joke.

Yeah never.

Which is probably a good reminder to go and clean out that 'nice' aspirational underwear drawer.

Yep, there is no way I'm going to get back into that French lace and silk set. However, I'm creative so maybe I could turn it into a patchwork silk and lace pillowcase. At least I'd have great hair and no wrinkles.

Back to that FaceTube page, dear diary.

COVID humour and mischief has seen some folks post spoof items on this page previously. The most memorable one was a picture of a filthy mattress that looked like it had been the scene of a massacre. It was offered for sale, $50. It was clearly a joke, which was admitted later, but again the comments were hilarious. The amount of people that took it seriously and were offended was more than a little funny. Which, of course, only amused me more.

I know the external readers only come for the scores on the doors, dear diary. Today NSW COVID cases total 623. Again, this is a heartening decrease.

Other heartening scores are 211,389 doses were administered nationwide on 2 October. This is nearly 100,000 down on normal daily doses but who wants to give up time on the weekend when you can take time off work? 16,364,525 people have had at least one dose. This is 66.09% of the total population or 79.36% of 16+

These percentages will decrease when vaccinations are opened to age 12 and over. 11,654,963 people are fully vaccinated. This is 45.37% of all Australians, or 56.52% of 16+. Again, these numbers will shift and decrease with the 12+ additions. Meanwhile in NSW, 88.4% of 16+ have had at least one dose and 67.1% have had two: so once more, "round again" class leader.

Okay it's a sunny day in Sydney so I'm going to move the catch-up work chore outside to the newly beautified balcony. It may be still in need of fairy lights and plants but catching up on work is more palatable sitting in the sun with fresh air, great views and limited traffic noise.

Until tomorrow dear diary. Until tomorrow.....

Lock-Down-Under - Day 102 – a week is a long time in politics

Geez dear diary,

How things change. On Friday we had a progressive, single little Premier with her ballet slippers and multiple jackets.

Only a few days later we have lost the premier, the Deputy Premier, presumably due to protests about his beard, and a Transport Minister. I swear I am frightened to go to sleep at night, who the hell knows what leadership changes I will wake up to? It's surreal, dear diary it really is.

What is also surreal is the questions some folks paste on FaceTube, except maybe not today as it's suffered a catastrophic failure, as has Insta and WhatsApp. I was particularly interested to see this little gem.

What's it like to date a Scottish lass?

And one of the answers? It's not bad, as long as you don't mind the odd bit of discharge.

Now in this context, I do know what he means. We passionate Scots females are very prone to discharge our verbal weaponry, in full automatic mode. Sometimes, well most times, it continues until the ammunition bank is empty. Which can take a fair wee while.

I am also informed that some precautionary measures for the male of the species are required. The first measure being to just bunker down for a day. Batten down the old hatches and wait out the Scottish Storm. However, this advice was from the same person who informed me that I was the JSF (Joint Strike Fighter or F35 as it's known by) of girlfriends.

- High Maintenance.
-
- High Risk.
-
- High Reward.

I seriously have never been sure if this is an insult or a compliment. So ever the optimist, it's a compliment.

Now then, on the high reward, the lockdown is having an effect. Finally!! Only 603 COVID cases in NSW today. Alas, though, the poor bloody Victorians with 1763 cases. Holy smoke.

The way ahead? Well, 138,537 doses were administered nationwide on 3 October. Again, this is about 200,000 less than normal. Long weekend, perhaps? NSW figures show that 88.5% of 16+ have had at least one dose and 67.5% have had two. You would think that in the next three weeks we would see a double dose over 80% but vax number are dropping off. Worrying as 80% was the magic number.

Okay back to the gulags dear diary. Until tomorrow.....

Lock-Down-Under - Day 103 – lies, lies and damn statistics!

Oh, dear diary,

You're late, you're late for a not very important date.

Yep, dear diary I know I am. This diary entry posting is about 7 hours later than usual due a variety of reasons. I went out for a couple of walks yesterday and worked my ass off in-between as for the first time in my life I am struggling to keep up with work. It's like hanging onto the roof of a Ferrari with a stuck accelerator and bad brakes. Look in a playful mood, I would have commented that a Ferrari is bad Italian shit and to go with German cars but, I'll let that one go to the keeper.

Back to my dilemma. When I got home from the delightful night walk last evening, I spent a pleasant hour doing food prep for the rest of the week. It's amazing how easy a salad is when all the ingredients are chopped and ready to throw delicately on a plate. Yeah, cos delicate, that's me! I spent some time considering what concoction of 'stuff' in my cupboard that I was going to use to marinade the chicken breasts I had cut into precise slices. Man, I've gone from something runny with pasta to chopping green and red stuff with gay abandon. No offense boys, adverb not noun!

Today was much the same. I got to work at 7am and at 5.45pm I was done; or done in. Exhausted and still nowhere near ready to say I was on top of my workload. It felt a little overwhelming. The safety of 1000 students in a COVID world with a return to school directive might do that!! So, I did what every tired, upset, battle weary, war veteran, twice divorced, financially astute woman does. I phoned my mum. Tell you what, the Oatmeal Savage is a saint among women. She doesn't read my daily diary posts, so am not worried that anyone will tell her!

The reason for the lies and statistics today is the cases were 584 but a delightful little graph on the ABC webpage says it's down 580, or maybe that was yesterday. We are also over 85% single dose and 70% double dose in NSW. Retail opens on Monday!!

Right now, its 7.45pm and after ploughing through a simply divine chicken salad and bribing myself with a second gin and tonic, I've moved to the study to do another hour or so of work. I have no doubt I'll work better half cut! Hic!

So, until tomorrow dear diary. Until tomorrow.….

Lock-Down-Under - Day 104 – the new walk of shame

Oh, dear diary,

How I miss the old days.

By the old days I don't mean when I was wetting the bed and begging my mum for food. No, dear diary, I mean further back than just three years ago! I am referring to the days when I'd be out all night and creeping home in the wee hours. Those days. Oh, how I miss them.

Those really were the times that one looks back on fondly. The days of Duran Duran, Soft Cell and Live Aid. The days of watching the boys walking home the next day wearing the same clothes from the night before and hoping nobody would notice. Yeah, right. We all noticed. We would also wonder where and which room they were coming from. But it's different now. The walk of shame is much different in lockdown and that was blatantly obvious this morning.

I took my early morning walk and arrived home to see one of the residents of my apartment complex sneaking shamefully to the bin room. He was holding two Uber Eats bags and one very large KFC Bag. I didn't know I could do that one raised judgemental eyebrow thingy, but I must have. I didn't think I had it in me. Surely on the Myers Briggs Type Indicator tests I'm not judgemental?? Moi? Non!! Yeah, like hell I'm not and it must have shown in that one look.

The poor bloke went scarlet with humiliation and stated. "Yeah, I'm embarrassed to do this most mornings! Always can't resist and it always disappoints" This is when we decided that at our age (he was about 31 too) the walk of shame differed with each decade. He continued to the Bin Room and I watched his very shapely legs like the Bitch in Heat I may very well be. Still having, thoughts about Hugh for about 104 bloody days now.

Anyway, some things are also decreasing (like my age) and that is the NSW COVID cases today, 587. Seven less than yesterday, so that'll do.

Until tomorrow, dear diary, when we may be down to 573 or something! Until tomorrow....

Lock-Down-Under - Day 105 - or FD minus three

Oh, hello dear diary,

Yep, this may be a Friday, dear diary and the start of a weekend but it's what's at the other end.

FREEDOM DAY.

It's been a long, long lockdown and I am ready to go visit a pub and drink, with friends, with strangers, with other things that breathe. Right now, I don't think I'm awfully fussy. I just want to go and see people. Any people.

It's been a short but exceptionally busy week and I know that as I've had to continually bribe myself with gin to go back to the computer each night. Maybe it'll calm down when we finally get kids back to school. This was a plan that changed yesterday when the new Premier brought some of the school returns forward a week. But my team are ready for it. I am also ready. I am ready to cope with the anxiety that people may face when pulled from their sofas, are required to take of their slippers and asked to come back into the office. A location with over one hundred other adults and close to one thousand students. This type of transition anxiety is something normally faced by Defence personnel coming home on completion of a deployment. Sometimes some of the side effects are hard.

I am confident that we will get through it. The good thing is that the school return date of 25 Oct is getting closer to Christmas. November is normally where the excitement starts. This is combined with the fact this is a nine-week term and not ten. All things that when communicated well, will hopefully bolster the humour and focus of our team.

Today's NSW COVID cases are 646. So once again an uprising.

Until tomorrow dear diary. Until tomorrow....

Lock-Down-Under - Day 106 – the penultimate day in captivity, new bookings accepted.

Oh, dear diary,

It's a glorious Saturday morning.

It started for me with a quick walk down to Bunnings to pick up another part in the jigsaw that is pimping up my balcony. The solar fairy lights. Like greased lightning, I was in and out of the shop, box in hand, back went I zipped to the Playgirl Penthouse.

An hour later the lights were unpacked, and the solar panel was positioned in the sunlight for the required six to eight hours of charging.
Yeah, that's where the wheels fell off. On placing all the lights around the green wall and checking the solar panel, I wasn't sure if I'd switched it on to charge. Bugger, seven hours of sun wasted.

Ah, well. This is Australia so no doubt it'll be sunny again tomorrow!

On the positive side, I've two dinners and a lunch already booked for next week! Oh, I can't wait. Somebody making and serving me dinner!

Oh, and btw, NSW COVID today has only 580 cases. Unlike our poor bloody neighbours down in Victoria. 1975 or so. More a good music year than a statistic really!

Until tomorrow rear diary. Until tomorrow.....

Lock-Down-Under - Day 107 - And so, the end is nigh.....

Scream!

Oh, dear diary,

Tomorrow is the end of lockdown.

I have two dinners and a lunch already booked it. I'm probably not alone in doing some pre bookings but I'm not as 'passionate' as some others! There are beauty clinics opening at midnight tonight because some of the NSW population are so desperate for their Botox injections that they will do overnight bookings! Does it make Botox react better if you can lay down and rest straight after the injection of God-knows-what into your forehead and frown lines??

So today, day 106 will be my last daily diary post. I was trying to think of something funny or some profound observations, but I've come up short. It could be the lack of Sunday afternoon alcohol! This has been an unusual time in my life; over 100 days of living alone and speaking to people via electronic means. Yes, there have been a few forays into work and to some essential shops but that's no substitute for actual human company.

In fact, on the few occasions I've seen friends, I've nearly killed them! Once with one of the teachers at school. I nearly squeezed the heart out of that little greyhound. The second time was two days ago, on Friday night when one of my lovely neighbours paid a surprise visit from his enforced recluse down on the snow. He's been hiding down there for three months! He's not quite as thin and is more muscular than the teacher at school but I swear I saw fear in his eyes when I wouldn't let him go!

The lovely thing is that now, he and his boyfriend are coming upstairs for drinks this afternoon! A nice start to freedom!

Anyway, NSW COVID today has only 477 cases. Who knows what the statistics will be when we open but 90% of NSW has had one dose and 75% has had two; so now we are relying on the pharmaceutical companies promises. After all that's why they are making millions and millions of dollars from these products.

Thanks for taking this journey with me and all your support. Strangely I started this to share my solo journey and feedback was always very welcome. And helpful; so, thank you all.

That's it dear diary, we are done! So, it's goodbye from me.....

Freedom is Mine

Free-Down-Under - Week One - first night madness

Oh, dear diary,

Memories, memories. What a delight they are. And how grateful we were that there were no camera phones.

How I have thought back to those old Navy and Air Force detachments this week. Oh man, how I remembered all those first nights. I have wondered how I survived them. And came out unscathed.

Oh, it's certainly been a week to remember!

It's a strange, wild thing that happens when military groups go away on exercise. Maybe it is the away from home opportunity. Maybe it's because there is a group of like-minded people. Maybe it's because you know that you have a few hard weeks in front of you. Maybe it's because you don't have to drive home. I don't know. But I do know the first night tends to be party night. First night madness or first night overspeed are the words used to describe this unofficial but very expected party.

And I have enjoyed parties all over UK, Europe and the US.

There has been dancing on bar tops in Vegas as well as a little bit of bus hijacking and an attempted water-skiing incident on an ironing board, 'trust me tours!' adventure walks home from German Clubs in Decimimanu, some dodgy bars in Waikiki and a very strange night or two in Shawbury, of all places. Once whilst still trying to look after my dog and ensure he was fed and walked.

All that history and I truly don't think any have rivalled the complete assault and blatant disregard of respect with which I have treated my body this week.

When I finished a nine-month deployment in Sudan, I had only had eight hours sleep in the final week. By the time I got on the plane from Khartoum to UAE, I was a broken woman.

Well, round again class leader! That was this week.

Apart from putting in some heavy 12 – 15-hour days at work with additional catch up this weekend, I've managed five dinners and more than a couple of lunches. Italian. Thai. Japanese. Sea Food. Gin and anti-pasta. I've done them all.

I am exhausted and am putting myself back into a self-imposed week of lockdown; immediately. I am done. A week of bread and water. Minus the bread.

Finally, finally, finally, in this week we reached 80% double dose vaccinations in NSW and the Government scrapped quarantine for Aussie residents. They also introduced a huge mental health initiative. Clearly recognising the toll this has had on people.

Now if they'd like to follow that up with a drunk tank, I'm your woman!

Thank you

Thank you for following my adventures during my COVID lockdown. It's taken two years for me to complete this book. Reading back on my thoughts and missives over the last few months have brought back some amazing memories, have generated a lot of laughter and in some cases a few tears, I still don't believe we are meant to be alone and locked up in our homes the way we were, but we were. And until now it seemed like a distant memory.

I hope you enjoyed the wildness that is Lee de Wanton, deWinton, de Winter, or whatever.

Printed in Great Britain
by Amazon

43389218R00096